*The Mystery at the Chalet School* was originally published in *The Chalet Book for Girls* in 1947. It is set just after *Jo to the Rescue* and before *Tom Tackles the Chalet School* and is known as no 19a in the series.

*Robin Heeds the Call* has been written by prize-winning author Sheena Wilkinson together with Susanne Brownlie, and edited by Tig Thomas. As the title suggests, this novella is about when Robin realises she has to answer God's call to be a nun. This could never be an easy book to write, but Sheena and Susanne have written with enormous sensitivity, and as EBD might have done.

GW01066297

# THE MYSTERY AT THE CHALET SCHOOL

ELINOR M BRENT-DYER

AND

# ROBIN HEEDS THE CALL

SHEENA WILKINSON AND SUSANNE BROWNLIE

Girls Gone By Publishers

COMPLETE AND UNABRIDGED

Published by
Girls Gone By Publishers
4 Rock Terrace, Coleford, Radstock, Somerset, BA3 5NF

First published by W & R Chambers 1947
This edition published 2014
Text and Chalet School Characters © Girls Gone By Publishers
Discovering the Chalet School Series © Clarissa Cridland 2002
Publishing History © Clarissa Cridland 2014
Note on the Text © Adrianne Fitzpatrick 2014
*Robin Heeds the Call* © Sheena Wilkinson & Susanne Brownlie 2014
Design and Layout © Girls Gone By Publishers 2014

Cover design by Ken Websdale
Typeset in England by Books to Treasure
Printed and bound by CPI Group (UK) Ltd, Croydon, CR0 4YY

ISBN 978-1-84745-180-4

The butler circled round the stage.

# CONTENTS

# DISCOVERING THE CHALET SCHOOL SERIES

In 1925 W & R Chambers Ltd published *The School at the Chalet*, the first title in Elinor Brent-Dyer's Chalet School series. Forty-five years later, in 1970, the same company published the final title in the series, *Prefects of the Chalet School*. It was published posthumously, EBD (as she is known to her fans) having signed the contract three days before she died. During those 45 years Elinor wrote around 60 Chalet School titles, the School moved from the Austrian Tyrol to Guernsey, England, Wales and finally Switzerland, a fan club flourished, and the books began to appear in an abridged paperback format.

## How Many Chalet School Titles Are There?
Numbering the Chalet School titles is not as easy as it might appear. The back of the Chambers dustwrapper of *Prefects of the Chalet School* offers a simple list of titles, numbered 1–58. However, no 31, *Tom Tackles the Chalet School*, was published out of sequence (see below), and there were five 'extra' titles, of which one, *The Chalet School and Rosalie*, follows just after *Tom* in the series chronology. In addition, there was a long 'short' story, *The Mystery at the Chalet School*, which comes just before *Tom*. Helen McClelland, EBD's biographer, helpfully devised the system of re-numbering these titles 19a, 19b and 19c.

Further complications apply when looking at the paperbacks. In a number of cases, Armada split the original hardbacks into two when publishing them in paperback, and this meant that the paperbacks are numbered 1–62. In addition, *The Mystery at the Chalet School* was only ever published in paperback with *The Chalet School and Rosalie* but should be numbered 21a in this sequence.

Girls Gone By are following the numbering system of the original hardbacks. All titles will eventually be republished, but not all will be in print at the same time.

Apart from *The Chalet School and Rosalie*, Chambers published four other 'extra' titles: *The Chalet Book for Girls*, *The Second Chalet Book for Girls*, *The Third Chalet Book for Girls* and *The Chalet Girls' Cook Book*. *The Chalet Book for Girls* included *The Mystery at the Chalet School* as well as three other Chalet School short stories, one non-Chalet story by EBD, and four articles. *The Second Chalet Book for Girls* included the first half of *Tom Tackles the Chalet School*, together with three Chalet School short stories, one other story by EBD, seven articles (including the start of what was to become *The Chalet Girls' Cook Book*) and a rather didactic photographic article called *Beth's Diary*, which featured Beth Chester going to Devon and Cornwall. *The Third Chalet Book for Girls* included the second half of *Tom Tackles the Chalet School* (called *Tom Plays the Game*) as well as two Chalet School short stories, three other stories by EBD and three articles. (Clearly the dustwrapper was printed before the book, since the back flap lists three stories and two articles which are not in the book.) It is likely that *The Chalet School and Rosalie* was intended to be the long story for a fourth *Book for Girls*, but since no more were published this title eventually appeared in 1951 in paperback (very unusual for the time). The back cover of *The Second Chalet Book for Girls* lists *The First Junior Chalet Book* as hopefully being published 'next year'; this never materialised. *The Chalet Girls' Cook Book* is not merely a collection of recipes but also contains a very loose story about Joey, Simone, Marie and Frieda just after they have left the School. While not all of these Chalet stories add crucial information to the series, many of them do, and they are certainly worth collecting. All the *Books for Girls* are difficult to obtain on the second-hand market, but most of the stories were reprinted in two books compiled by Helen McClelland, *Elinor M. Brent-Dyer's Chalet School* (out of print) and *The Chalet School Companion* (available from Bettany Press). Girls Gone By have now published all EBD's known short stories, from these and other sources, in a single volume.

## The Locations of the Chalet School Books

The Chalet School started its life in Briesau am Tiernsee in the Austrian Tyrol (Pertisau am Achensee in real life). After Germany signed the Anschluss with Austria in 1938, it would have been impossible to keep even a fictional school in Austria. As a result, EBD wrote *The Chalet School in Exile*, during which, following an encounter with some Nazis, several of the girls, including Joey Bettany, were forced to flee Austria, and the School was also forced to leave. Unfortunately, Elinor chose to move the School to Guernsey—the book was published just as Germany invaded the Channel Islands. The next book, *The Chalet School Goes to It*, saw the School moving again, this time to a village near Armiford—Hereford in real life. Here the School remained for the duration of the war, and indeed when the next move came, in *The Chalet School and the Island*, it was for reasons of plot. The island concerned was off the south-west coast of Wales, and is fictional, although generally agreed by Chalet School fans to be a combination of various islands including Caldey Island, St Margaret's Isle, Skokholm, Ramsey Island and Grassholm, with Caldey Island being the most likely contender if a single island has to be picked. Elinor had long wanted to move the School back to Austria, but the political situation there in the 1950s forbade such a move, so she did the next best thing and moved it to Switzerland, firstly by establishing a finishing branch in *The Chalet School in the Oberland*, and secondly by relocating the School itself in *The Chalet School and Barbara*. The exact location is subject to much debate, but it seems likely that it is somewhere near Wengen in the Bernese Oberland. Here the School was to remain for the rest of its fictional life, and here it still is today for its many aficionados.

## The Chalet Club 1959–69

In 1959 Chambers and Elinor Brent-Dyer started a club for lovers of the Chalet books, beginning with 33 members. When the club closed in 1969, after Elinor's death, there were around 4,000 members worldwide. Twice-yearly News Letters were produced, written by Elinor herself, and the information in these adds fascinating, if sometimes conflicting, detail to the series. In 1997 Friends of the Chalet School, one of the two fan clubs existing today, republished the News Letters in facsimile book format. Girls Gone By Publishers produced a new edition in 2004.

## The Publication of the Chalet School Series in Armada Paperback

On 1 May 1967, Armada, the children's paperback division of what was then William Collins, Sons & Co Ltd, published the first four Chalet School paperbacks. This momentous news was covered in issue Number Sixteen of the Chalet Club News Letter, which also appeared in May 1967. In her editorial, Elinor Brent-Dyer said: 'Prepare for a BIG piece of news. The Chalet Books, slightly abridged, are being reissued in the Armada series. The first four come out in May, and two of them are *The School at the Chalet* and *Jo of the Chalet School*. So watch the windows of the booksellers if you want to add them to your collection. They will be issued at the usual Armada price, which should bring them within the reach of all of you. I hope you like the new jackets. Myself, I think them charming, especially *The School at the Chalet*.' On the back page of the News Letter there was an advertisement for the books, which reproduced the covers of the first four titles.

The words 'slightly abridged' were a huge understatement, and over the years Chalet fans have made frequent complaints about the fact that the paperbacks are abridged, about some of the covers, and about the fact that the books were published in a most extraordinary order, with the whole series never available in paperback at any one time. It has to be said, however, that were it not for the paperbacks interest in the Chalet series would, in the main, be confined to those who had bought or borrowed the hardbacks prior to their demise in the early 1970s, and Chalet fans would mostly be at least 40 and over in age. The paperbacks have sold hundreds of thousands of copies over the years, and those that are not in print (the vast majority) are still to be found on the second-hand market (through charity shops and jumble sales as well as dealers). They may be cut (and sometimes disgracefully so), but enough of the story is there to fascinate new readers, and we should be grateful that they were published at all. Had they not been, it is most unlikely that two Chalet clubs would now be flourishing and that Girls Gone By Publishers would be able to republish the series in this new, unabridged, format.

Clarissa Cridland

# ELINOR M BRENT-DYER: A BRIEF BIOGRAPHY

EBD was born Gladys Eleanor May Dyer in South Shields on 6 April 1894, the only daughter of Eleanor (Nelly) Watson Rutherford and Charles Morris Brent Dyer. Her father had been married before and had a son, Charles Arnold, who was never to live with his father and stepmother. This caused some friction between Elinor's parents, and her father left home when she was three and her younger brother, Henzell, was two. Her father eventually went to live with another woman by whom he had a third son, Morris. Elinor's parents lived in a respectable lower-middle-class area, and the family covered up the departure of her father by saying that her mother had 'lost' her husband.

In 1912 Henzell died of cerebro-spinal fever, another event which was covered up. Friends of Elinor's who knew her after his death were unaware that she had had a brother. Death from illness was, of course, common at this time, and Elinor's familiarity with this is reflected in her books, which abound with motherless heroines.

Elinor was educated privately in South Shields, and returned there to teach after she had been to the City of Leeds Training College. In the early 1920s she adopted the name Elinor Mary Brent-Dyer. She was interested in the theatre, and her first book, *Gerry Goes to School*, published in 1922, was written for the child actress Hazel Bainbridge—mother of the actress Kate O'Mara. In the mid 1920s she also taught at St Helen's, Northwood, Middlesex, at Moreton House School, Dunstable, Bedfordshire, and in Fareham near Portsmouth. She was a keen musician and a practising Christian, converting to Roman Catholicism in 1930, a major step in those days.

In the early 1920s Elinor spent a holiday in the Austrian Tyrol at Pertisau am Achensee, which she was to use so successfully as the first location in the Chalet School series. (Many of the locations in her books were real places.) In 1933 she moved with her mother and stepfather to Hereford, travelling daily to Peterchurch as a governess. After her stepfather died in November 1937 she started her own school in Hereford, The Margaret Roper, which ran from 1938 until 1948. Unlike the Chalet School it was not a huge success and probably would not have survived had it not been for the Second World War. From 1948 Elinor devoted all her time to writing. Her mother died in 1957, and in 1964 Elinor moved to Redhill, Surrey, where she died on 20 September 1969.

Clarissa Cridland

# PUBLISHING HISTORY

*The Mystery at the Chalet School* was first published in *The [First] Chalet Book for Girls* in 1947. As was to be the case with *Tom Tackles the Chalet School* (published in two parts in *The Second Chalet Book for Girls*, 1948, and *The Third Chalet Book for Girls*, 1949), the story was illustrated by W Bryce Hamilton, who, as can be seen from his illustrations, clearly had not read any of the Chalet School books—or at least had not taken note of the clothing worn! We have reproduced his black-and-white illustrations throughout this book. The colour frontispiece from *The Chalet Book for Girls* has been reproduced on the back cover and also, in black and white, as  our frontispiece. We have adapted the cover of *The Chalet Book for Girls* (there was no wrapper) for our cover, simply altering the title and removing 'edited by' above the author's name. The spines of all the *Books for Girls* were plain blue with white lettering, so we have not shown this on the back of our cover.

    *Mystery*, like *Tom*, was also reprinted by Murrays Sales & Service Co in 1970, in the unlikely publication *My Treasure Hour Bumper Annual* (shown opposite). In this annual *Mystery* was given contemporary illustrations which we have included as an appendix in this book.

It is interesting to note that the Contents page of *The Chalet Book for Girls* gives the title of this story as *The Mystery of the Chalet School*. The story header shows the title as *The Mystery at the Chalet School*. The updated story header in *My Treasure Hour Bumper Annual* has *The Mystery of*, yet the Armada edition uses *The Mystery at*.

*Mystery* remained out of print until, in 1994, Armada published it in a paperback edition together with *The Chalet School and Rosalie* (which sequentially comes after *Tom*). This had a preface by Helen McClelland explaining where the book should come in the series. The paperback was published at £3.50.

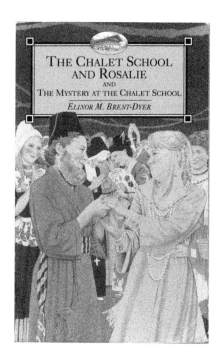

The first Girls Gone By paperback edition was produced in 2004. For this latest edition we have included a long short story by Sheena Wilkinson and Susanne Brownlie.

Clarissa Cridland

## NOTE ON THE TEXT

We have taken our text from *The Chalet Book for Girls*. We have inserted missing quotation marks, corrected the word order 'was even of more importance' to 'was of even more importance' (p64); and added a missing word: 'four people from the Lower Fourth' has become 'and four people from the Lower Fourth' (p113).

Adrianne Fitzpatrick

# COMPLETE NUMERICAL LIST OF TITLES IN THE CHALET SCHOOL SERIES

(Chambers and Girls Gone By)

Dates in parentheses refer to the original publication dates

1. *The School at the Chalet* (1925)
2. *Jo of the Chalet School* (1926)
3. *The Princess of the Chalet School* (1927)
4. *The Head Girl of the Chalet School* (1928)
5. *The Rivals of the Chalet School* (1929)
6. *Eustacia Goes to the Chalet School* (1930)
7. *The Chalet School and Jo* (1931)
8. *The Chalet Girls in Camp* (1932)
9. *The Exploits of the Chalet Girls* (1933)
10. *The Chalet School and the Lintons* (1934) (published in Armada paperback in two volumes—*The Chalet School and the Lintons* and *A Rebel at the Chalet School*)
11. *The New House at the Chalet School* (1935)
12. *Jo Returns to the Chalet School* (1936)
13. *The New Chalet School* (1938) (published in Armada paperback in two volumes—*The New Chalet School* and *A United Chalet School*)
14. *The Chalet School in Exile* (1940)
15. *The Chalet School Goes to It* (1941) (published in Armada paperback as *The Chalet School at War*)
16. *The Highland Twins at the Chalet School* (1942)
17. *Lavender Laughs in the Chalet School* (1943) (published in Armada paperback as *Lavender Leigh at the Chalet School*)
18. *Gay From China at the Chalet School* (1944) (published in Armada paperback as *Gay Lambert at the Chalet School*)

19.   *Jo to the Rescue* (1945)

19a.  *The Mystery at the Chalet School* (1947) (published in *The Chalet Book for Girls*)

19b.  *Tom Tackles the Chalet School* (published in *The Second Chalet Book for Girls*, 1948, and *The Third Chalet Book for Girls*, 1949, and then as a single volume in 1955)

19c.  *The Chalet School and Rosalie* (1951) (published as a paperback)

20.   *Three Go to the Chalet School* (1949)

21.   *The Chalet School and the Island* (1950)

22.   *Peggy of the Chalet School* (1950)

23.   *Carola Storms the Chalet School* (1951)

24.   *The Wrong Chalet School* (1952)

25.   *Shocks for the Chalet School* (1952)

26.   *The Chalet School in the Oberland* (1952)

27.   *Bride Leads the Chalet School* (1953)

28.   *Changes for the Chalet School* (1953)

29.   *Joey Goes to the Oberland* (1954)

30.   *The Chalet School and Barbara* (1954)

31.   (see 19b)

32.   *The Chalet School Does It Again* (1955)

33.   *A Chalet Girl from Kenya* (1955)

34.   *Mary-Lou of the Chalet School* (1956)

35.   *A Genius at the Chalet School* (1956) (published in Armada paperback in two volumes—*A Genius at the Chalet School* and *Chalet School Fête*)

36.   *A Problem for the Chalet School* (1956)

37.   *The New Mistress at the Chalet School* (1957)

38.   *Excitements at the Chalet School* (1957)

39.   *The Coming of Age of the Chalet School* (1958)

40.   *The Chalet School and Richenda* (1958)

41.   *Trials for the Chalet School* (1958)

42. *Theodora and the Chalet School* (1959)
43. *Joey and Co. in Tirol* (1960)
44. *Ruey Richardson—Chaletian* (1960) (published in Armada paperback as *Ruey Richardson at the Chalet School*)
45. *A Leader in the Chalet School* (1961)
46. *The Chalet School Wins the Trick* (1961)
47. *A Future Chalet School Girl* (1962)
48. *The Feud in the Chalet School* (1962)
49. *The Chalet School Triplets* (1963)
50. *The Chalet School Reunion* (1963)
51. *Jane and the Chalet School* (1964)
52. *Redheads at the Chalet School* (1964)
53. *Adrienne and the Chalet School* (1965)
54. *Summer Term at the Chalet School* (1965)
55. *Challenge for the Chalet School* (1966)
56. *Two Sams at the Chalet School* (1967)
57. *Althea Joins the Chalet School* (1969)
58. *Prefects of the Chalet School* (1970)

**EXTRAS**

*The Chalet Book for Girls* (1947)
*The Second Chalet Book for Girls* (1948)
*The Third Chalet Book for Girls* (1949)
*The Chalet Girls' Cook Book* (1953)

# COMPLETE NUMERICAL LIST OF TITLES IN THE
# CHALET SCHOOL SERIES
(Armada/Collins)

1. *The School at the Chalet*
2. *Jo of the Chalet School*
3. *The Princess of the Chalet School*
4. *The Head Girl of the Chalet School*
5. *(The) Rivals of the Chalet School*
6. *Eustacia Goes to the Chalet School*
7. *The Chalet School and Jo*
8. *The Chalet Girls in Camp*
9. *The Exploits of the Chalet Girls*
10. *The Chalet School and the Lintons*
11. *A Rebel at the Chalet School*
12. *The New House at the Chalet School*
13. *Jo Returns to the Chalet School*
14. *The New Chalet School*
15. *A United Chalet School*
16. *The Chalet School in Exile*
17. *The Chalet School at War*
18. *The Highland Twins at the Chalet School*
19. *Lavender Leigh at the Chalet School*
20. *Gay Lambert at the Chalet School*
21. *Jo to the Rescue*
21a. *The Mystery at the Chalet School* (published only in the same volume as 23)
22. *Tom Tackles the Chalet School*
23. *The Chalet School and Rosalie*
24. *Three Go to the Chalet School*
25. *The Chalet School and the Island*

2

# NEW CHALET SCHOOL TITLES

In the last few years several authors have written books which either fill in terms in the Chalet School canon about which Elinor did not write or carry on the story. These are as follows:

*Chalet School World*—short stories by Helen Barber, all written specially for this book. The first is set just before Joey is born, and the last is in the late Swiss era. (Girls Gone By Publishers 2013)

*The Chalet School Christmas Story Book* edited by Ruth Jolly and Adrianne Fitzpatrick—featuring short stories by Helen Barber, Katherine Bruce, Caroline German, Heather Paisley and more (Girls Gone By Publishers 2007; out of print)

*The Bettanys of Taverton High* by Helen Barber—set immediately before *The School at the Chalet*, covering Joey's last term at her English school (Girls Gone By Publishers 2008; out of print)

*The Guides of the Chalet School* by Jane Berry—set in the gap between *Jo of the Chalet School* and *The Princess of the Chalet School* (Girls Gone By Publishers 2009)

*Juliet of the Chalet School* by Caroline German—set in the gap between *Jo of the Chalet School* and *The Princess of the Chalet School* (Girls Gone By Publishers 2006; out of print)

*Deira Joins the Chalet School* by Caroline German—set in the gap between *Jo of the Chalet School* and *The Princess of the Chalet School* (Girls Gone By Publishers 2010)

*Visitors for the Chalet School* by Helen McClelland—set between *The Princess of the Chalet School* and *The Head Girl of the Chalet School* (Bettany Press 1995; Collins edition 2000)

*The Müller Twins at the Chalet School* by Katherine Bruce—set in the gap between *Jo Returns to the Chalet School* and *The New Chalet School* (Girls Gone By Publishers 2012)

*Gillian of the Chalet School* by Carol Allan—set between *The New Chalet School* and *The Chalet School in Exile* (Girls Gone By Publishers 2001; reprinted 2006; out of print)

*The Chalet School and Robin* by Caroline German—set after *The Chalet School Goes to It*. The 2012 edition includes a short story: 'Joey and Jean'. (Girls Gone By Publishers 2003; new edition 2012)

*A Chalet School Headmistress* by Helen Barber—set during the same term as *The Mystery at the Chalet School* (Girls Gone By Publishers 2004; out of print)

*Peace Comes to the Chalet School* by Katherine Bruce—set in the gap between *The Chalet School and Rosalie* and *Three Go to the Chalet School*; the action takes place during the summer term of 1945 (Girls Gone By Publishers 2005; out of print)

*A Difficult Term for the Chalet School* by Lisa Townsend—set between *Three Go to the Chalet School* and *The Chalet School and the Island* (Girls Gone by Publishers 2011)

*New Beginnings at the Chalet School* by Heather Paisley—set three years after *Prefects of the Chalet School* (Friends of the Chalet School 1999; Girls Gone By Publishers 2002; reprinted 2006; out of print)

# FURTHER READING

*The Chalet School Encyclopaedia Vol I* by Alison McCallum (Girls Gone By Publishers 2013)

*Behind the Chalet School* by Helen McClelland (essential)*

*Elinor M. Brent-Dyer's Chalet School* by Helen McClelland. Out of print

*The Chalet School Companion* by Helen McClelland*

*A World of Girls* by Rosemary Auchmuty*

*A World of Women* by Rosemary Auchmuty*

*Available from:
Bettany Press, 8 Kildare Road, London E16 4AD, UK
(http://www.bettanypress.co.uk)

# The Mystery at the Chalet School

BY

ELINOR M. BRENT-DYER

# CONTENTS

# ILLUSTRATIONS

# The Mystery at the CHALET SCHOOL

The Chalet School pupils had returned after the summer holidays to find the school possessed of a full-fledged mystery in the shape of Dorcas Brown, a new girl. Not that Dorcas looked like a mystery at first sight. She was really quite ordinary, with mousy-brown hair, eyes that might be called grey by courtesy, a pink-and-white face, and features similar to those which are found in the faces of two-thirds of the girls of any school. Neither was she anything 'to shout about' in the way of lessons, as Gay Lambert expressed it.

'Well, you *should* know!' half a dozen voices had chorused when Gay had said this.

Gay shrugged her shoulders. 'In our family, the brains go to the boys. My sister Ruth never was much at lessons, and I'm like Ruth. So it's not much use my fussing, is it?'

'You never did, my lamb!' laughed Mollie Avery; and this was almost an insult, for Mollie had just scraped into Upper Fifth by the skin of her teeth.

Gay shrugged her shoulders again, but said nothing. She was

feeling very disgruntled at the moment, for her great chum, Gillian Culver, had headed the list which left Lower Fifth for Upper, and by the end of the first fortnight had worked her way up to third in that form. But then, besides being clever, Gillian was hard-working, and Gay, to be quite frank, was neither.

The rest, with some understanding of how she was feeling, left the subject, to turn again to that of the new girl.

'The queerest thing about her is the way she "dries up" if you even mention her home or her people,' said Barbara Henschell. 'The rest of us talk about our folk quite a lot—I'm sure you people know all about our crowd at home—but she rarely does.'

'I know,' chimed in Peggy Burnett. 'And if she does, she stops short just as it's beginning to get interesting, and tries to change the subject. I've noticed it lots of times.'

'So've I,' agreed Gay, perching herself on one of the desks—they were in their form-room at the time—and crossing her ankles. 'I was telling her about Ruth and Tommy and the babies the other day when she was my partner for the walk. I was saying how really lovely Ruth is, and how sorry we are that her little Nan doesn't take after her. She said was I like Ruth at all? Of course, I told her we weren't in the least alike in looks, though awfully so in brains. She said, "But you are pretty yourself, you know, Gay."' Here Gay stopped, and went red. 'Well, that's what she said—awful rot, of course!'

'Rubbish!' said Peggy ruthlessly. 'Don't pretend, Gay. You know you're one of the prettiest girls in the school. You'd be an ass if you didn't!'

'Besides, you didn't make yourself,' put in big, untidy Frances Coleman wistfully. 'Madame would say you'd no right to crab your own looks.'

'Oh, well! Anyhow, Dorcas said, "I've always thought it would be so nice to be pretty. When you're the only plain one in the family, it's a bit of a drop. *My* sister is a dream to look at." Well, of course, I asked her what she was like—you know she hasn't a single photo in her cubey—and she said, "Oh, lovely!"'

'That wasn't telling you much,' put in Marie Varick.

'No; was it? But when I tried to get some details from her, she just laughed and said her sister really was lovely, but I couldn't be interested in a stranger, and when did I think we'd begin hockey. And she wouldn't say another word about it.'

'That's the way she spoke to me,' said Roosje Lange, a Dutch girl of their age, who was a very pretty person herself. 'I was telling her on Sunday about all our babies, and she said that she was the baby of their family. Well, naturally, I asked her how many of them there were, and she said: "Oh, only my sister and I." Then she muttered something about getting a book to read, and got up and left, and she didn't come near me for the rest of the afternoon.'

'She's queer,' said Peggy firmly.

And there they had to leave it.

As the term went on, they saw no reason to change their belief. Pleasant enough in school, and always ready for a gossip about school affairs, Dorcas always shut up like a clam, to quote Gay, when anything was said about her home or her people. All they knew of her was that her family was in America, and that was something she couldn't have hidden, for letters from America came for her every week or so.

'Are you American?' Gay once asked her.

'Of course not,' said Dorcas. 'We're as English as you are.'

'I suppose your Dad's over there on business,' said Gay, speaking mainly from friendliness.

'Yes. Oh yes,' said Dorcas hurriedly. Then she asked, 'What do you think of that awful Virgil we have to do? I can't find a solitary predicate in any of the first fifteen lines. Can you?'

Gay was, of course, promptly led away. But later on she remembered it, and added it to the list of 'queer things' she had noticed about the new girl.

'We've had some rummy folk here,' she said to her other great friend, Jacynth Hardy, a shining light of Upper Fourth, 'but I do think that Dorcas is one of the oddest in some ways.'

'I don't know much about her,' said Jacynth, who certainly made up for Gay's laziness, since she worked whenever it was possible. 'I thought she looked quite nice. But none of our crowd has seen much of her. You ought to be chums, Gay. You've been bracketed in form-lists both last fortnight and the one before.'

Gay laughed. 'Oh, I'm going slow so that you can get up to me. Then we'll go ahead together. What did Miss Burnett say about your being second last time? That was a jolly good effort for a new form, old thing.'

Jacynth's pale face flushed. 'She said, "Congratulations, Jacynth. If you go on like this, we'll have to see about promoting you to Lower Fifth next term." I wish they would! I'd love to be with you, Gay.'

Gay shot her a quick glance. Jacynth had only come to the Chalet School the previous term from a very small private school where the girls had been well grounded and taught how to work, but the curriculum had been much smaller than that of the Chalet School. Jacynth had known no Latin, and had been weak in mathematics, so she had been placed in a somewhat low form. But already she had earned her promotion to Upper Fourth, and she was aiming at Lower Fifth at the earliest opportunity.

The pair had met on the train going to school. Gay had made friends with the new girl at once, and stood by her through the first weeks of a life quite different from any she had previously known. Later in the term, when Jacynth had lost the aunt who was her sole relative, and who had brought her up from babyhood, it had been Gay who had helped her to bear the loss. Jacynth had spent the summer holidays with Gay and the married sister with whom she made her home, since Gay's mother and brothers lived with an uncle in China; and the Lamberts had done all they could to make the lonely girl feel that she was not left homeless and friendless in the world.

'You'll do it, old thing,' said Gay, slipping her arm through Jacynth's with a quick, chummy squeeze. 'In fact, I shouldn't be in the least surprised if you went ahead and got into Upper Fifth before me.'

Jacynth's somewhat sad face broke into a smile. 'Don't talk rot, Gay. If I do get into Lower Fifth next term, you've got to keep level with me—'

'Not on your life!' cried Gay, using forbidden slang in her horror. '*I'm* no slogger, and not even you could reform me at this late date; so I warn you!'

'We'll see,' was all Jacynth would say.

'What are you going to see about?' demanded a fresh voice; the two turned as the third member of their triumvirate, Gillian Culver, walked into the room.

'Transforming Gay into a slogger,' said Jacynth firmly. 'But it shouldn't need all that, Gay. You aren't *batty*, you know.'

'I'm not brainy, and never will be,' said Gay. 'Gill, what do you think of Dorcas Brown?'

'She's a queer stick,' said Gillian thoughtfully. 'I quite like what I know of her. But that's uncommonly little.'

'You probably know as much as any of us,' said Gay. 'She's not too bad at work, and she plays quite a good game at hockey. Her manners are all right—I mean, she has just the same sort as the rest of us, and doesn't go in for any fancy frills like some of our foreign people. Neither does she eat peas with a knife.'

'How do you know that?' asked Jacynth with a grin. 'We haven't had peas this term.'

'I was speaking metaphorically,' said Gay with dignity.

'Swallowed a dictionary,' observed Gillian with a wicked glance at Jacynth. 'You might have looked after her better in the "hols," Jac.'

'Well, I like that!' cried Gay. 'You're always jumping on me for talking slang. But if I try to use decent English, you rag me about swallowing a dicker!'

'There's a gentle mean, Gay, my lamb.'

'Oh, stop scrapping, you two!' said Jacynth. 'As for Dorcas Brown, she's a plain mystery in some ways. But if she wants to keep her home dark, it's her own business and nothing to do with us.'

This common-sense view of the question ended the talk. Gay and Jacynth went off to separate music-rooms to put in a little 'cello practice, and Gillian, who was not specially musical, retired to her own form-room to wrestle with an article on British seabirds, which, in a rash moment, she had promised Gwensi Howell, the school editor of *The Chaletian*.

The trio did not meet again till after supper, when there was dancing in the Hall for those who wished; the rest could amuse themselves in the Senior common-room. Gillian and Gay were both good dancers, but Jacynth had not learned till she came to the Chalet School, when various people had insisted on teaching her to waltz, one-step, and also perform the Valeta, barn dance, and the Lancers. In addition, the girls had folk-dancing once a week and enjoyed it. Various people took it in turns to provide the music, and although there was always a select few who preferred the quiet of the common-room and books, needlework, or table games, most of the Seniors were generally to be found disporting themselves in Hall after supper.

'As for Dorcas Brown, she's a plain mystery.'

They were left pretty much to themselves, as the authorities believed in trusting the girls. Any mistress who did come in was certain to be mobbed by eager partners, but it was understood that they were there strictly unofficially, and the head-girl and prefects were responsible for what went on.

On this occasion they had been dancing some twenty minutes when the door quietly opened, and a tall, slim person, with black hair wound in huge plaits on either side of a clever, sensitive face, came in and stood to one side, watching the long lines of 'Mary and Dorothy.' Daisy Venables, a member of Lower Sixth, was the first to see her, and she broke from the ring, leaving her partner and opposites gasping as she dived through the dancers to the far side of the room, exclaiming, 'Joey! What ever brings *you* here at this time?'

'Hello, Daisy,' said the newcomer, putting an arm round the slim shoulders, and bending her head to kiss the fresh face lifted to hers. 'I meant to be here for tea, but it didn't come off. The new Vicar and his wife called at four, so I couldn't in decency send them away unfed, and they sat and sat till half-past six, by which time, as you very well know, I had all my work cut out to get my family off to bed by seven.'

By this time, the dance had come to a full stop, and the dancers were literally mobbing 'Joey,' all asking questions at once, and chattering, till she suddenly yelled, 'Stop it, all of you! I can't hear a thing! Now then,' as a hush gradually fell on the Hall, 'what is it you want to know? Why haven't I been up before? Well, didn't you know that we've all been in quarantine for chicken-pox? Margot began it; but the other two followed on the next day. Only Stephen escaped—for which I was thankful. He's got quite enough to do with cutting his teeth as it is. Luckily, they all had it as lightly as they could, and they're all quite well now, thank you.'

'I didn't say anything,' said Daisy. 'Miss Wilson thought it best not. Prim and I hadn't really been near the babes, and besides, we've both had it, as you very well know. The mark's on my nose yet!' And she squinted violently in her efforts to glimpse the tiny dint left after the illness.

'If you go on doing that, you'll stick that way permanently,' warned Joey. 'It would be no improvement, let me tell you. Stop it, Daisy!'

'We thought you must still be away, Mrs Maynard,' said Gillian.

'Not I! I've been ministering to my young! And that brings me to my reason for landing up here after seven. I *must* have my termly party, even though it's so late in the term. So I want all the new Seniors to come to tea on Saturday if possible. Who's Games Prefect this time? You, Jocelyn? Well, what about it? Is there a match?'

'Yes; but it's an away one,' said Jocelyn Redford, a pleasant-looking girl with thick reddish hair drawn back in a long pigtail. 'It's with Cron-y-bach, Mrs Maynard, so only the team and the reserves will be going. It's too far for the rest.'

'Oh? Good luck to the team! Mind you beat them! But that means only walks or "friendlies." So that'll be all right for my party. Who are the new girls? Bring them up and present them, someone.'

Laughing, the girls seized on the half-dozen or so new Seniors and brought them to her. They were introduced by the head-girl, Jesanne Gellibrand, a small, dark girl with an interesting face.

'This is Dorothea Wentworth in Upper Fifth, and this is Dorcas Brown in Lower Fifth. And these four are all Upper Fourth: Margaret Jones, Jean McGregor, Anthea Barnett, and Anne Walker. The other new girls are mainly Juniors or Babies, and are in bed.'

'I'll see them another time,' agreed Mrs Maynard, flashing a smile round the little group of new girls. 'Well, you people, it's rather late to say it, but welcome to the Chalet School. And now I hope you'll all come to tea with me on Saturday, and bring a friend with you. The others will explain to you that this is the usual thing each term, only, as you've heard, I've been coping with chicken-pox in my large family and couldn't come near you.'

'Thank you very much,' said Dorothea Wentworth, taking the lead as the oldest there. 'We should love to come.'

'Then that's settled! Oh no, my child!' as Jesanne invited her to join in the dancing. 'I've got to get back. I'll come to a Saturday if I may—a "soon" Saturday, please. I'm going away for a few days presently, when Dr Maynard can get off. And after that you'll all be busy with the Christmas play, as you very well know. I'll just bag Daisy for a few minutes if you can spare her.'

'Take her and welcome!' said Jesanne laughingly. 'Come any Saturday you like, Mrs Maynard. It's our turn next week. What about then? We're having refreshments,' she added with a chuckle.

'Provided Steve is all right, I'll come with pleasure.'

'Bring him with you,' suggested Gwensi Howell. 'If he's yelling with his teeth, we can take it in turns to carry him about.'

'Thank you, Gwensi. That's quite a bright idea—except that if it's done once, he'll expect it to be done every time. However, I think the bothering one will be through in a day or two's time, and then we should have peace for a while. Come, Daisy-girl!' And with a laughing nod she went out, her arm round Daisy, and the door was shut.

'Who is Mrs Maynard?' asked Dorcas Brown of Gay Lambert as they took partners for a polka.

'She's—well, she's Mrs Maynard,' said Gay. 'I know that sounds mad, but it's rather difficult to express. Lady Russell, who owns this school, is her sister, and Joey was a pupil when the school was in Tirol. And she's never really left in one way. She's married, of course, and she has a family—her girls are triplets, and then there's Stephen, who is getting on for a year—but she's always kept coming back.' She caught at Jesanne Gellibrand, who was passing them at that moment. 'Half a tick, Jesanne! Come and tell Dorcas just what Joey Maynard is to us, will you?'

Jesanne stopped. 'She's the spirit of what the school is meant to be,' she said gravely. 'At least, that's what most of us feel. But you must get to know her, Dorcas. Then you'll see what I mean,' as she saw the look of blank bewilderment on Dorcas's face.

'There's one thing I *can* tell you,' said Gay. 'She's Josephine M. Bettany.' She paused expectantly, but the cry she had expected from Dorcas was not forthcoming.

'Ought I to know her?' asked the latter doubtfully.

'Ought you to know her? Where *was* you riz?' demanded Gay. 'Do you mean to say you've not read any of her books?'

'I haven't heard the name until you mentioned it.'

With a laughing nod she went out, her arm round Daisy.

'But where on earth have you been *living*?'

'Oh, here and there,' said Dorcas airily. 'Go on; tell me what books she's written. I may have read them. I never pay much attention to authors of books.'

Somewhat flatly, Gay replied, 'Oh, she wrote, *Cecily Holds the Fort*, and *Nancy Meets a Nazi*, and *The Leader of the Lost Cause*. That was her latest, and it's glorious, though it's a historical novel—all about the Forty-Five, you know. The others are books for girls.'

'*The Leader of the Lost Cause*?' cried Dorcas. 'But that's—' She stopped abruptly. Then she went on, 'That's almost the last book I read before coming to school. I liked it so much.'

'*That* wasn't what you were going to say,' said Gay bluntly.

Dorcas reddened. 'It's all I *want* to say, anyhow!' she snapped.

Gay stared at her in silence for a moment. 'We'd better dance,' she said curtly. 'Come on!'

But later on in the dormitory, she told Jacynth and Gillian of the episode—strictly in confidence—and demanded to know what they thought of it.

'Awfully queer,' said Gillian. 'Have you any idea what she meant, Gay?'

'Not I! But there's something very much secret about that girl, and I'd like to know what it is.'

# *Chapter II*

## QUEERER AND QUEERER!

Joey Maynard's tea-party came off in due course, and the six new Seniors were escorted to Plas Gwyn, the Maynards' pretty if rambling old house, which stood just outside Howells Village. In accordance with time-honoured usage, each had an 'old' girl with her. Dorcas, told what was expected of her, promptly invited Gillian to come. There had been a little coolness between her and Gay ever since the evening when Mrs Maynard had come with her invitation. However, Gillian had already promised Dorothea Wentworth, so Dorcas had to fall back on Gay after all. Jacynth was Jean McGregor's chosen friend, so the triumvirate—the second triumvirate in the school, as Daisy Venables had once remarked, she and her two chums, Gwensi Howell and Beth Chester, being the first—were together, much to their glee.

Mrs Maynard had provided progressive games with a prize for the first part of the time. This was won by Jean, who was presented with a copy of *The Secret House*, one of Mrs Maynard's own books. As she was a Josephine Bettany 'fan,' already owning six of that lady's works, she was delighted, and went about for the rest of the time in a sort of solemn ecstasy. Then came tea, and afterwards a formal visit to the nursery to meet the Maynard triplets and Joey's splendid baby boy. The girls were then sent down to the drawing-room once more to play paper games, while Joey saw to Stephen's bath, and had the new girls one at a time for a little chat.

By this time, that lady had heard from Daisy Venables, who

was her 'niece-by-marriage,' to quote Daisy herself, all about the strange new girl, and she was especially interested in her.

But although Dorcas chatted willingly enough about school, she said nothing of her own affairs, and Joey, who had already heard all about Dorothea's younger sister Frances, who would follow her sister to the Chalet School as soon as she was fourteen, and Jean's quiet little home in Edinburgh with her professor father and matter-of-fact, hustling mother, and how Jean herself wanted to write books some day, rather wondered. However, she was wise enough to keep her wonderings to herself, and asked no questions, much to the relief of her guest.

Stephen was in bed by this time, and it was the turn of the triplets, who were three enchantingly pretty little girls, with very much the same features, though they were quite unlike in colouring.

'Now, then, you three!' said their mother warningly as she came into the nursery. 'Bed-time!'

'Oh, *need* we?' mourned Margot, the youngest of the triplets.

'I'm afraid so, my precious. Girls who have had chicken-pox have to be very careful about going to bed early for a few months.'

'Can we be later when that's over?' asked Len, the eldest, eagerly.

'We'll see,' said Joey prudently. 'Come along and get undressed. Say good-night to Dorcas first, though.'

The three came up to the girl, holding out their hands.

'Good night,' said Len. 'Thank you for coming.'

Con, the dark member of the triplets, smiled. 'It's so nice to see all the new girls,' she said as she shook hands daintily.

Margot gave *this* new girl a wicked glance from eyes as blue as forget-me-nots. 'Hopes we'll see you again,' she said.

Dorcas laughed. 'I hope so, too,' she said as she shook hands. She would have liked to kiss the three, but they had plainly no idea of that. Later, she found that, while kisses and cuddlings were all a part of their daily home-life, they were most sparing with their caresses, and rarely offered them to strangers.

Joey, looking on laughingly, caught a queer look in the eyes of the new girl. It was such an unexpected look, that she was almost inclined to think she had imagined it.

'It was almost as though—as though she was *judging* them for a very particular reason,' she thought as she whisked them off to the night-nursery, bidding Dorcas run downstairs and tell Margaret Jones to come up in about twenty minutes' time. Then she shook herself. 'Oh, what nonsense! I must be going batty in my old age!' Sad to relate, Mrs Maynard not infrequently both thought and spoke in schoolgirl language, though she *could* be dignified enough on occasion.

Meanwhile Dorcas went downstairs to send Margaret up to the nursery at the appointed time, and then joined in the uproarious game of 'New Novels' which the girls were playing.

'Well, what do you think of our nursery folk?' asked Daisy, who was with them.

'Jolly, aren't they?' said Dorothea. 'And how pretty they all are!'

'They're alike in one way, but not in another,' said Jean.

Daisy nodded. 'They're unlike in more ways than one, as you'd soon find if you lived with them. Len tries to keep them all in order, but it's a hard life with a monkey like Margot about.'

'They're just sweet, I think,' said Anthea eagerly. 'Wouldn't they make a lovely picture if they were painted together?'

'Wouldn't they be lovely on a film?' suggested Anne Walker.

Daisy shook with laughter. 'I'd be sorry for any producer who had to tackle them! However, there isn't the faintest chance of it ever happening—not as long as they are children, anyhow. Of course, later on one of them may take it into her head to want to become a film star, but I'm sure I hope not. I think it must be a ghastly life. Everyone knowing all about you, and having to answer millions of fan-letters every week! Appalling!'

'Oh, but you'd have a secretary for that,' said Dorcas eagerly.

'I suppose you would. But still, I'm sure Joey wouldn't want a life like that for one of her girls. However, they're only babies yet—not four till next month—so we needn't worry about them.'

'But don't you have to begin young?' asked Anne doubtfully.

'I don't know. I don't know much about it at all,' said Daisy. 'Come on! Let's get on with our game. Where had we got to?'

The subject dropped, and they went on with the game. Joey had Anthea after Margaret, and then sent for Anne. By that time the triplets had had their supper, said their prayers, and were safely tucked up in bed; the nursery had been tidied up. Joey came down to announce that her guests had but half an hour before they must leave to catch the bus that ran past the end of the lane leading to Plas Gwyn, and to ask what they would like to do.

'You haven't sung to us,' said Jacynth. 'You will, won't you?'

'Oh, yes, you must sing!' exclaimed Gillian. 'It won't be a properly rounded-off party if you don't.'

'There's no one to accompany me,' began Jo.

'Yes, there is,' said a new voice from the door. '*I'm* here! Hello, everyone. How's school?'

With a shriek of '*Robin!*' all the 'old' girls rose and flung themselves on the girl who stood in the open doorway. She fended them off with outstretched hands, and when everyone was calm again, came in, briskly demanding to be introduced. The new girls were named to her by Joey, who wound up with, 'And this is my sister, Robin Humphries, who is home for the week-end from Oxford.'

'She was at school last term,' cried Gay. 'Robin, what is Oxford like?'

They flung themselves on the girl who stood in the doorway.

'Very jolly. You ought to make up your mind to come, too,' said Robin calmly.

'Talk sense! A lot of use I should be there!' retorted Gay. 'Besides, I can't. I'm going to take up 'cello good and hard once I've got through School Cert. I want to be a professional 'cellist.'

'Jo had better introduce you to our new friend Phoebe Wychcote at that rate,' said Robin. 'Her father was Nicholas Wychcote, and she's at the San. at present, undergoing treatment for rheumatism. You heard Nicholas Wychcote, I'm sure. He died only about two years ago.'

'I should think I did hear him! That was what made me work really hard at Cerita'—Gay's pet name for her 'cello—'I've always felt I'd like to play as well if I only could. Is Miss Wychcote really near here—and your friend? Robin, introduce me if you ever get the chance! I'd love to meet her!' coaxed Gay.

'You'll do that all right,' said Joey. 'She's marrying Dr Peters at the San. in December, and they are going to live in Ty-Gwyn, that little house next to Frieda von Ahlen's. So you're bound to meet her.'

'How—how *sumptuous*!' sighed Gay.

'You and your old Cerita!' said Daisy with friendly scorn. 'We want to hear Joey sing. Go on, Rob; choose something for her.'

Robin laughed, and went to the piano. Mrs Maynard followed her.

'I'll sing one song of my own choice and one of yours,' said the lady cheerfully. 'What's it to be, Gill?'

'What's your own choice?' asked Gillian cautiously.

'Bach—"Jesu, Joy of Man's Desiring." Now what's yours?'

'That song of Elgar's, "Where Corals Lie," please. I love it.'

Robin sat down, and struck a chord. 'I can play that from memory. Gill asks for it every single time she's given a choice. Get down to it, Joey!'

While the girls sat silent, Joey Maynard stood by the piano and sang the song with a voice as sweet and effortless as a bird's. She possessed no very great power, but every note rang out with a bell-like clarity and roundness that was as much the result of a wonderful gift as careful training. She followed it with her own choice, and then it was time to get into hats and coats and say goodbye.

On the bus Dorcas sat silently, while the rest chattered like magpies. She was reviewing the party to herself.

'I nearly gave things away twice,' she thought. 'I simply *must* be more careful. I'm not going to have all the fuss I had at my last school. It was too awful! It would be frightfully easy to let something slip, and some of these girls are like needles. But I promised everyone I'd hold my tongue, so I must. What a piece of luck to meet Mrs Maynard like this! I never should have dreamed of its happening. Now I must try to get really friendly with her. Then—well, then, if it's humanly possible, I'll have a good hard go at her and try to make her change her mind. That would please Eunice more than anything. Mother and Father, too. Eu told me it was her very greatest wish. I should just love to get it for her. I must think what's the best way to go to work about it, for I certainly can't miss a chance like this!'

She was roused from her reverie by the stopping of the bus to let them get out. It was dark, of course, but a mistress was waiting to escort them up the long avenue to Plas Howell with a torch, and they all carried their own, having been forewarned by Matron when she had reviewed them before they went off.

'Did you enjoy it?' asked Gay as they paired off for the walk.

'Yes, very much,' said Dorcas. 'How beautifully Mrs Maynard sings!'

'Yes, doesn't she! Daisy once told me that she'd always been able to sing, though she'd had the best training she could

A mistress was waiting to escort them with a torch.

get. It isn't a big voice, but it's so sweet and—well—*unearthly*, somehow.'

'It reminded me of something I once heard Daddy say,' said Anne Walker, who was just behind with one Esme Béranger, her chosen friend. 'He's an organist, you know, at the parish church of Leston. Years ago when I was a tiny, they gave "The Dream of Gerontius" in the church—the Leston Choral Society and the choir. They had one of the "big people" down to sing the Angel, and when it was over, I was out with Daddy next day, and we met some friends of his, and they were talking about the concert. Daddy said about the Angel, "She wasn't a singer—just a Voice, floating in something-or-other space. There was nothing human about it." Well, I felt like that about Mrs Maynard.'

'It doesn't sound quite—canny,' said Gay, 'but I see what you mean.'

Then they reached the second gates. Miss Linton called on them to hurry as the bus had been late and supper would be over before they got in if they loitered. The conversation ceased.

Meanwhile, at Plas Gwyn, Jo was sitting down to supper with Robin Humphries, her husband, and the young Dr Peters, who was to marry Phoebe Wychcote in a few weeks' time.

'How did the party go off?' asked the doctor as he served the kedgeree.

'Very well, I think. They seem a nice set of girls.'

'Do you know, Jo,' said Robin, 'it's a queer thing, but one of them struck me as being vaguely familiar? I don't mean I've ever actually met her, but I seemed to know her face.'

'Who was that?' asked Joey.

'Dorcas Brown, I think they called her.'

'Dorcas Brown? Well, so far as I know we've not had anyone called Dorcas Brown in our very varied acquaintance,' said Jo. 'In fact, when I come to think of it, the only other Brown whom I have known was that old Miss Browne who started St. Scholastika's School at the other side of the Tiernsee. D'you remember her, Rob?'

Rob gave a shriek of laughter. 'Do I *not*! How wild you and Dick and Papa were when she stopped you that first day she was there, and tried to snaffle you for a pupil! But this Dorcas child isn't a scrap like that, so you can put that episode out of your mind, Jo, my child.'

'Oh, I didn't think the long arm of coincidence could be stretched as far as that,' said Jo with an involuntary chuckle. 'Perhaps it's someone you've met at Oxford.'

Robin shook her head. 'Nothing like that.' She screwed up her face in the effort to remember.

'I did not realise,' said Jo, looking at her with interest, 'how really plain you *could* look, Rob. Indeed, between Daisy squinting to try to see the end of her nose, and the awful faces you are making at the present moment, I seem to be surrounded by *gargoyles*! Go on with your supper, and leave it alone. Making faces isn't going to help you to remember anything. But you can tell me if it ever comes to you,' she added with renewed interest. 'Daisy declares that that girl is an "unsolved mystery," for she won't say a thing about her home or her people; and though school has been going for nearly five weeks now, they know no more about her than they did in the beginning.'

Robin giggled, and her face resumed its normal beauty, while Jo changed the subject by telling Dr Peters about Gay and Jacynth and their 'cellos, and Gay's latest ambition. No more was said about Dorcas Brown for the time being.

# Chapter III

## THE MYSTERY DEEPENS

O h, Dorcas! Have you heard what's going to happen at half-
term for everyone who isn't going away?'

Dorcas looked up from her algebra. 'No. Is it anything very exciting?'

Gay flopped down on a chair beside her. 'What are you doing? Oh, algebra! Isn't it awful? I loathe problems! But about the half. Well, there won't be many of us left—only twenty-five or so, as lots of people are going home with chums. The mistresses on duty are Miss Burnett and Miss Linton, and Miss Edwards for the Babies. Even Bill is going to be away, because she's going to stay with Miss Annersley—'

'Who's she?' interrupted Dorcas.

'The Head, of course!'

'The Head? I thought Bill was that?'

'No; she's acting-Head at the moment, but the real Head is Miss Annersley. Didn't you know? They were hurt—Bill, and the Abbess and Miss Edwards and Mlle Lachenais—in a ghastly motor accident at the end of the Easter holidays. Bill broke her leg, and so did Miss Edwards, only rather worse. Mlle smashed an arm and had a fearful bruising as well. But they're all right, though they have to be careful still about doing energetic things. But the Abbess was struck on the head. She nearly died. She is very frail still, and won't come back for ages yet. But she's done with hospitals now, and is living with a cousin in a house not far from Chepstow. So Bill's going to see her. Miss Burnett will be in charge. Well, she was talking to the prees who are staying—there are only two of them, Kitty Burnett and Clare Danvers—and Kitty was telling Daisy, who told me, that on the Monday we are going to the cinema in Armiford to see that film with the new star in it. "Tedder's Cove" it's called. Isn't that gorgeous? Usually they won't let us get so much as a sniff at a cinema during term-time. But this is historical, and Miss Burnett says we ought to see it, because it will give us such a good idea of what life in England was like during the Napoleonic wars.'

Gay was so interested in her subject, that she did not notice the change in the face of the new girl when she heard the name of the film they were to see. Dorcas had first flushed and then gone white. Her lips closed firmly, and her eyes darkened. But she said nothing.

'We're going to the balcony,' Gay chattered on. 'That's to give us no chance of catching anything, of course. And they're booking tables in the cinema café. Isn't it gorgeous?'

'It'll be—fun,' said Dorcas rather faintly. Then, 'Oh, Gay, do go away and let me get this done! I haven't finished *one* yet, and there are three to do! Miss Slater will be furious if I don't show up a bit more than this.'

'Don't worry, my child! By the time she's finished with me she'll be so exhausted that she won't have breath to slay anyone else.'

Dorcas laughed, but she turned resolutely to her rough-book. Gay, seeing she was determined, left her, and went to find someone else to whom to tell the news.

Alone, the new girl pushed algebra and rough-book to one side, and sat staring unseeingly out of the window. This was something she had not expected. What was she to do? She would have loved to see the film; but in the circumstances she felt the only safe thing was to stay away. But could she possibly manage that?

'I must say nothing just yet,' she decided as the bell rang for preparation and the others began to come into the room. 'Then, on the day I must just have a headache. I can't think of anything else.'

'Dorcas Brown!' exclaimed Gay, pausing beside her at this point. 'Do you mean to say you've got no more of that algebra done in this last half-hour?'

'I don't seem able to see through it,' stammered Dorcas, closing her book. 'I'll give it up and do the rest, I think. Perhaps I may be able to do better when I come back to it.'

Gay eyed her sharply. 'Aren't you well?'

'Yes—at least, my head aches a little. No, Gay! You aren't to tell Matey. It's nothing! I'll be all right presently.'

'You've slogged too much at that old algebra,' scolded Gay.

'Perhaps I have. I'll give my *Merchant* a turn. I like learning by heart, you know.'

Dorcas took her *Merchant of Venice* out of the desk, and set herself to learn Salarino's speech to Antonio in the first scene. After that, she went at the rest of her work with grim doggedness, even tackling the algebra during the final half-hour, and managing to get the first two problems worked out, though she could make nothing of the third. By this time her head was aching in good earnest, and she was thankful when the bell brought preparation to an end, and she could put the books away in her desk. No one but an examination candidate was ever allowed to work after supper at the Chalet School. Dorcas's lack of appetite at supper could not go unnoticed, and Matron took her in hand the moment the meal ended.

'Dorcas Brown, aren't you well?'

'Just a little headache,' said Dorcas. 'It isn't anything, Matron—*really*.'

'Come up to my room,' said Matron inexorably.

The girls might try to coax with some of the mistresses, but even Joey Maynard, who had always been Matey's darling, had

'Come up to my room,' said the Matron.

not attempted to wheedle her. Matron was little, but she was a tyrant if it were necessary. Even Miss Wilson and Miss Annersley had been known to bow before her edicts. Dorcas went meekly upstairs and submitted to having her tongue looked at, her temperature taken, and swallowing a dose of some mixture Matron usually administered for minor ailments. Then she was ordered to go to bed, which she did more thankfully than Matron knew.

Those people who were staying at school for half-term were full of excitement over the prospect of a trip to the cinema, especially as it was to see the new star, Eunice Brownlow, whom most of them had seen in her previous film, and greatly admired.

'Aren't you thrilled?' Jacynth asked Dorcas on the Thursday when they were putting their books away at the end of afternoon school.

Dorcas laughed. 'I don't know that I am. I've been such heaps of times to the flicks that I can't feel awfully excited.'

'I've been very few times,' said Jacynth with a glance back over the years when she and Auntie had been obliged to think before they spent even sixpence unnecessarily. Her little pointed face under the thick mass of springy dark hair grew suddenly grave, and Dorcas wondered at it.

'Don't your people approve?' she asked, a certain hardness edging her tone.

'It wasn't that,' said Jacynth simply. 'We couldn't afford it.'

Dorcas stared. 'But it doesn't cost all that much.'

'We had to think before we spent. I must go and practise.' And Jacynth vanished, leaving the new girl still wondering.

Gay and Gillian came into the room together a few minutes later, and she promptly tackled them on the subject.

'I say, you two, I want to know something,' she began.

'Carry on, then,' said Gay amiably.

'Jacynth has just been telling me she didn't go to the flicks because she couldn't afford it. But this isn't what you'd call a *cheap* school. I saw the prospectus when Daddy sent for it. Did she win a scholarship or anything?'

'No,' said Gillian quickly, before Gay could reply. 'Besides, you mightn't want to waste money on movies, but would do a lot to give your girl a decent education. That's what Jacynth's aunt did. It matters, you know, Dorcas.'

'Does her aunt not go to the cinema?'

'Jacynth's aunt died during last term,' said Gillian gravely. 'Don't say anything to her about it, Dorcas. It was a big loss.'

'Well—I just don't understand. Whatever did Jacynth do for fun if she didn't go to the flicks?'

'Oh, she had her share of fun,' said Gillian. 'And she enjoys life now, even if there is a kind of shadow on things.'

'Oh,' murmured Dorcas, and left the topic. But she went on to something which was of even more importance to her. 'Do *you* go?'

'At home? Not often. We live right out in the country, so it means doing a matinée as a rule, and even then it isn't always convenient.'

'We don't go an awful lot, either,' said Gay. 'It isn't easy for Ruth to park the babes anywhere, and she couldn't leave them. There'd be no house to come back to if she did! Nan is a good little thing, but young Bobby is the limit! He beats even my twin and me for wickedness.'

'Don't you approve of flicks, then?' asked Dorcas eagerly.

'I don't either approve or disapprove,' said Gillian. 'They're good fun once in a way. But I'm not cinema-mad. There are other things I like much better.'

'I wouldn't mind if they didn't have canned music,' said Gay. 'Some of it is so awful and cheap it sets my teeth on edge. I like a movie now and again. It'll be a real treat on Monday.

And as it's historical, they *can't* shove in a lot of ghastly swing music—so-called—although I suppose we'll have to put up with it between-whiles.'

'Don't worry,' said Gillian. 'Daisy says Robin Humphries has seen it, and it's a whole show in itself. There'll only be the newsreel besides.'

'Oh, it's a fearfully long picture, even now,' agreed Dorcas. 'And they cut it all to pieces after it was first made.'

Gay looked up with interest. 'How on earth do you know that?'

'Oh, I—I read about it in a magazine or somewhere,' said Dorcas, flushing as she spoke.

'There's a magazine in the common-room with photos from it,' said Gillian suddenly. 'Stills, don't they call them? Let's go and bag it after tea, and then we'll get some idea of what to expect.'

'Right you are!' said Gay, shutting down her desk-lid with a bang, and jumping to her feet. 'There! I've finished for five glorious days! Come on, you two! I hear the tea-bell ringing! Where's young Jacynth got to, I wonder?'

'She said she was going to practise,' said Dorcas, as she got up from her desk.

'She's mad about her 'cello. She's playing awfully well for a beginner. I rather think Mr Manders intends to take her on after half-term,' said Gay. 'He said last time that he expected she was ready for him now. *And* he congratulated me on having had to stop to think just why and how I did things! It's done me pounds of good—I know that!'

Then they left the room and went to the dining-room, which looked painfully empty with just two tables laid, most of those who were going away for the week-end having gone during the afternoon.

Jacynth came in to tea late, but rules were always relaxed at half-term, so no one said anything. Only Dorcas noticed that Gay plied her with bread-and-butter and the slabs of currant cake that were by way of being a treat. When tea was nearly over, the door opened, and Miss Burnett and Miss Linton came in. They were both old girls of the school, and great friends. The girls liked both, though they were so different, for Miss Burnett was a short, stocky person, of whose looks the most that could be said was that she had a pleasant face, while Miss Linton was tall and slight, and very pretty, with black hair, blue eyes, and apple-blossom colouring. She was a Junior mistress, and Miss Burnett took history throughout the school with the exception of the Kindergarten.

They were greeted by a chorus of welcomes.

'Come along!' said Kitty Burnett, jumping up. 'We're delighted to see you.' And she grinned impishly at the history mistress, who was her eldest sister. In lesson-times Kitty was very punctilious about addressing her sister and Miss Linton as 'Miss Burnett and Miss Linton.' Out of them, and when they were alone, she reverted to old times, and they were 'Mary' and 'Gillian' to both her and Peggy, the third of the Burnett girls.

Miss Burnett grinned back at her. 'Even half-term doesn't give you too much licence, my child,' she said, as she sat down.

'No, of course not. But have you come to tell us our programme?'

'Just that. Tonight, we thought as you are all so tired with hard work—naturally—we wouldn't do anything out of the ordinary. You can dance in the Hall if you like, or you can read or play games. We'll be delighted to join you if you'll invite us.'

'Oh, rather! Do come!' Clare Danvers said quickly.

'Thank you very much. Most of the staff have gone off already, and Miss Wilson is only waiting for the car to come for her, since she isn't allowed to drive yet, so the Staff-room is somewhat empty.'

'Like this,' said someone cheerfully.

'Exactly. For tomorrow we propose a long walk in the morning if it's fine, taking sandwiches with us and getting tea somewhere, so that we needn't hurry to get home for dinner. We can take our own tea and mugs, and we're sure to find someone who will boil a kettle for us. We ought to be back by four, as the dark comes so soon now. After tea, I don't suppose anyone will want to be very strenuous if we have a really long walk, so that it would be a good idea to get on with the scrapbooks for the children's ward at the Sanatorium.'

'And if we do that,' put in Miss Linton, 'the Babies can join in. Miss Edwards is taking them off to the Round House for the early part of the day as there are only seven of them, and Madame has invited them to go and play with Josette.'

'Then that settles them,' said Gillian Culver. 'What do we do on Saturday, Miss Burnett?'

'On Saturday we're all going over to Medbury for the day. We'll look round the town—there's some lovely old black-and-white work for you to see there—and then we'll go on to Malvern after lunch, have tea there, and come back. In the evening, we'll dance and play nursery games after supper for the Babies. Sunday we'll have church, of course. As we are so few, we thought we'd go to the village church for once if it's fine. Walk in the afternoon, and reading as usual at night. Monday is the Armiford trip, and we're taking you round the cathedral in the morning, having lunch at Mrs. Lucy's, and tea at the cinema café. Tuesday morning, we'll leave free for anything that turns up. The rest will be back by tea-time, you know. Now how does that suit you all?'

'Splendidly, thank you,' said Kitty. 'Have you had tea?' she added, looking doubtfully at the big urn standing in solitary state on a side-table.

'Ages ago! Thank you all the same. Well, you'd better all go and change into your frocks for the evening, and then we'll join you in the Hall in about half an hour's time.'

They carried their cups and plates to the buttery hatch, and when the tables were cleared, scattered to the dormitories to change into their velvet frocks for the evening. Gillian and Gay were soon ready, and Jacynth was not far behind them.

'You go down and I'll go and see if Dorcas is ready,' proposed Gay. 'Go and bag that mag. you talked of, Gill, and let's see what we're in for on Monday, shall we?'

'All right,' agreed Gillian. 'Come along, Jac.' She led the way along the corridor to the stairs.

On the way they were joined by Clare Danvers and Peggy Burnett, a shining light of Upper Third. In the Hall were two or three others, while Miss Edwards had the seven Kindergarten babies in a corner and was telling them a story which provoked peals of laughter from them. Two or three of the elder girls gravitated to this group, for Miss Edwards was a notable teller of stories. The rest moved on to the common-room, where Gillian made a swoop on her magazine, opened it, and found on the middle page the pictures of which she had spoken.

'Here we are!' she said. 'This is "Tedder's Cove." Oh, what a pleasant village! Look, Jacynth!'

'That's Eunice Brownlow,' said Jacynth, pointing to a picture of a pretty girl in long, hooded cloak, with the hood pulled over her carefully dishevelled curls. Large eyes looked out from beneath finely arched brows, and the sensitive lips were barely parted in a smile.

'I like her,' said Jacynth. 'She hasn't got that awful, *toothy* grin so many of them seem to have. But—it's really funny—I seem to know her. Don't you, Gill?'

'Know her?' said Gillian in surprise. 'I thought you said you hadn't seen her before?'

'Well, I certainly didn't see her first picture—you know, the one about Charles I. But she looks familiar, all the same.'

Dorcas pushed it aside. 'I'm sick of the stupid flick!' she burst out.

The two girls scanned the pictures closely. Finally Gillian nodded. 'You're quite right, Jac. She *is* familiar. I haven't seen "Cavalier's Daughter" any more than you have, but I'm sure I know her face. Where on earth can I have seen her?'

Gay and Dorcas came in at this moment, and the former exclaimed, 'I thought we'd find you here! Come on, you two. Dancing's just going to begin. Oh, are those the pictures? Let me see! Oh, what a lovely girl! Look, Dorcas!' She held out the magazine.

To the surprise of the other three, Dorcas pushed it aside. 'I'm *sick* of the stupid flick!' she burst out, and turned and ran from the room.

They stood staring after her. Gay was, characteristically, the first to recover.

'*Well!*' she exclaimed. 'What do you know about *that*?'

## Chapter IV

## THE FLICK

The triumvirate spent the rest of the evening in a state of complete mystification about Dorcas. *Why* should she be so queer about a picture of a charmingly pretty girl, and why should she be so plainly upset at the idea of going to a flick?

Dorcas kept clear of them, though she need not have feared any questioning, for Gillian had contrived to get her chums into a corner and warn them to say nothing to her.

'But why not?' demanded Gay, who was given to pouring forth whatever happened to be on her mind at the time.

But Gillian was not only older in years, she was considerably more grown-up in her outlook on life, and she made them promise.

'It's only one more queer thing about her, I suppose,' said Gay. 'All right, Gill. You needn't preach. We won't say a thing.' Dorcas was left alone to her thoughts, whatever they might be.

The various arrangements for the other days helped to fill their minds to the exclusion of Monday, until Sunday came. Then, in the afternoon when they were all sitting quietly in the common-room reading, since the rain was coming down in full force, Gay pulled up her chair to Jacynth's, and said, 'Jac!'

Jacynth lifted her eyes from her book to ask, 'What?'

'Put your book down a moment. I want to talk.'

'When don't you?' demanded her friend, nevertheless laying down John Oxenham's *Scala Sancta*, which she was devouring with deep interest. 'Well, what is it?'

'It's about Dorcas, of course. Look here, Jac!' She produced the magazine. 'Look at that picture of Eunice Brownlow.'

Jacynth obediently looked at it. 'What about it?'

'Well, you said she reminded you of someone.'

'I didn't. I said she looked familiar.'

'Oh, well, it's much the same thing. I've found out whom she looks like.'

'Who is it, then?'

'Dorcas Brown, of course.'

'Dorcas Brown? Don't be so silly! This girl is lovely, and you couldn't call Dorcas even pretty. Gay, you're imagining things!'

'I'm not! Where's Gill? *She'll* see it if you can't.'

'She went upstairs to get a hanky. Here she is. Show her your picture and she'll tell you you're completely batty,' jeered Jacynth. 'Hi, Gill! Come here!'

Gillian came across the room. 'Matey was up there and caught me. Luckily, it's half-term Sunday, so she didn't say anything. What do you want, Jacynth?'

'Gay says that the reason why we feel we've seen Eunice Brownlow before is because Dorcas Brown is like her. Come and tell her she's batty. She'll be thinking one of us is like—like the Queen next!'

Gillian stood looking down at her with a curious smile. 'So Gay's seen it, has she? I wondered if either of you would.'

'*Gill!*' Jacynth suddenly snatched the magazine from Gay's hand and studied the picture carefully. 'Gay, I do believe you're right. Dorcas isn't a bit pretty, of course. In fact, you'd almost call her plain. But you're right. She *has* got a look of her! How weird! I say, I'm sorry I called you batty. But it seemed such an unlikely thing. I see now you were quite right.'

'D'you think that's why she doesn't want to see the flick?' asked Gay seriously. 'For, you know, she doesn't. But *why*?'

71

Gillian shook her head. 'I've no idea. If it's her sister or cousin or something, I should have thought she'd have been proud of her. I know I should if it had been Merle or Cherry, though I must say,' she added, 'I can't imagine Merle, at any rate, being any sort of an actress. Cherry might if she felt like it.'

'I suppose she *is* a relation?' said Jacynth doubtfully.

'When they're so alike? It couldn't be an accident, you know.'

'No; I see that. What are we going to do about it?'

'Nothing,' said Gillian gravely. She pulled up a chair and sat down, setting her elbows on her knee and resting her chin on her doubled-up fists. 'I don't know why she should take this attitude, but as she has, then we can only let it alone. Don't say anything to her, Gay. She must have some sort of reason, and you won't do any good by teasing her.'

'Teasing? As if I would!' cried Gay indignantly. 'But I won't even mention the subject since you're so much against it, Gill.'

'I didn't mean I thought you'd tease on purpose,' said Gillian. 'You're a bit of an ass sometimes, Gay, but I've never known you to be unkind. Only you are an awful gadfly occasionally. So I'm just warning you.'

It was not in sunshiny Gay to sulk, so she only nodded. 'All right. We'll let the whole thing alone. And I'm sorry for Dorcas if she really doesn't want to go,' she added. 'I don't see how she can get out of it. Neither Miss Burnett nor Miss Linton will leave her alone, and you know Teddy is off to spend the day with the Abbess and Bill. She said so when we were walking to church this morning. Matey's going with her, so there will be nobody but the maids here. I can't see any of the Staff leaving a girl alone with just the maids.'

In her quiet corner at the far side of the room, Dorcas was realising this for herself. If she carried out her first plan of pretending to have a headache, it would mean that someone would have to stay with her. What on earth could she do? It began to look as if she must just set her teeth and go with the others, and hope that they would not notice anything.

'But if they do,' she thought, 'and if there's all the fuss there was at Bentley Hall, I don't know what I shall do. Oh, if only I'd been pretty and gifted, too! But I'm just a dud, and I'm not going to dangle on anyone's tails, neither Eunice's nor anyone else's!'

That night, when they went to bed, she studied her face in the mirror. Then she took up a comb, combed all the front part of her hair forward, and picking up her scissors, calmly cut it to her chin. That done, she hunted in a drawer till she found a piece of broad elastic, which she fastened round her head. With this aid, she cut herself a fringe as evenly as she could. Then she stared at herself once more and nodded.

'That's better! It *does* make a difference! Now what can I do with that tail?' picking up the long strands of hair she had just cut.

She tucked it away in a drawer finally. Then, putting on her band again to persuade the fringe to stay in place, she undressed and got into bed, where she fell asleep, satisfied that it was most unlikely that anyone would notice her likeness to the young film star who had made such a sensation with her first picture.

Dorcas herself made a sensation the next morning when she appeared at breakfast, though it was indeed one of another kind. The first to get the benefit of her sudden change of hair-dressing was Clare Danvers, who ran into her at the head of the stairs, stared at her in complete bewilderment, and then demanded, 'Who are you—oh, good gracious! It's Dorcas Brown! You awful child! What possessed you to play such a trick?'

'I—I've been having headaches,' stammered Dorcas, her self-possession suddenly oozing out at her finger-tips. 'I had it cut once before when I was a kid.'

'Well, but to do it without asking anyone!' gasped Clare.

'Here! You'd better come to Matey—oh, bother! You can't! She and Teddy went off at eight. Well, come to Miss Burnett, then. But you've got to see *somebody*!' And grasping Dorcas's wrist, she marched her off down the corridor to the side one where the mistresses' bedrooms were, and tapped at Miss Burnett's door.

'Come in!' came that young lady's cheerful tones. 'Good gracious, Clare! What's wrong? And— *Dorcas Brown!*'

'What's Dorcas done?' asked Gillian Linton's merry voice as she came out of the next-door room. But she, too, stopped and gasped when she caught sight of the metamorphosed Dorcas. 'Dorcas Brown! You naughty girl! What possessed you to do such a thing?'

Rather frightened now, Dorcas proffered the excuse she had made to Clare.

'But if your head ached so badly, why didn't you tell Matron?' demanded Miss Burnett.

'Good gracious, Clare! What's wrong?'

Dorcas had nothing to say to that. She stood with her eyes cast down, twisting her fingers, and scarlet with mixed feelings. The two mistresses looked at her, then exchanged a glance of despair.

'Well,' said Miss Burnett rather flatly at last, 'it's done, and it certainly can't be undone at present. But I am very much annoyed with you, Dorcas. You are far too big a girl to play such a stupid trick as this, and if it weren't that it would mean someone staying too, I'd leave you behind today. You'd better go down to breakfast now. You can see Miss Wilson tomorrow about this.'

She turned and went into her room again, and Miss Linton followed her, leaving Clare to walk off and Dorcas to follow since she could think of nothing else to do.

Needless to state, there was an outcry when the new girl entered the room, and she was besieged by questions as to why she had cut her hair. Gay was not among the questioners. After her first exclamation of, 'Mercy, Dorcas! What *have* you been and gone and done?' she was silent, thanks to a sharp kick administered by Gillian. Jacynth, too, said very little. She had been suddenly seized with the memory that today was Auntie's birthday, and was lost in a dream of that last birthday when she had, with infinite pains, made a cake the week before, and produced it as a surprise for tea, as well as the girdle cakes which were a *sine qua non* for a birthday tea in their old home. Now Auntie was sleeping in the old churchyard of St Matthias, and all she could do for her was the cluster of chrysanthemums that Gay's sister Ruth had undertaken to place on the grave that morning. Jacynth nearly choked over her porridge.

Gay glanced at her, remembered what day it was, and slipped her fingers into Jacynth's cold ones with a loving squeeze. Jacynth returned it, swallowed the lump in her throat as well as she could, and went on with her breakfast.

'Go and make your beds, girls,' said Miss Burnett when Grace had been said. 'Mind you leave your cubicles tidy. You must be ready for the school bus at ten, so you haven't much time to waste. Off you go! And be sure you put your scarves on. The wind has a nasty nip in it, even though the sun *is* shining.'

They scattered, and in the necessary scurry to get the beds made and themselves ready in time, there was little chance of talking. But when they were in the school bus, Dorcas was once more beset by questions as to *why* she had done such a thing.

'Lavender Leigh did it in Easter term. Remember?' asked one of the Juniors.

'Yes, but that was *all* her hair,' said Peggy Burnett. 'Why did you cut yourself a fringe, Dorcas? What *will* Matey and Bill say when they see you?'

'Please speak of the mistresses by their proper names, Peggy,' said her sister severely from the back of the bus. 'And you can drop the subject, all of you.'

With Miss Burnett speaking like that, no one dared say anything more, and Dorcas was a thankful girl for that. When the bus dropped them by the old cathedral, where they were welcomed by a friend of the school who was to take them round, there was plenty to occupy their minds. It was half-past twelve before they came out again, and then they had to set off to walk to the Lucys' house in Weonister Road at the other side of the city. They were in good time for lunch, as Mrs Lucy informed them serenely when she came to meet them, Barney, her youngest boy, a sturdy urchin of four, mounted on her back, and little Viola, just five, driving them before her with yells. The rest of the family, Julie, John, and Betsy, came to welcome the guests with yells just as loud, for Julie and Betsy were at the Chalet School, and John was home from his prep. school for half-term, too.

'Let Julie and Betsy come with us,' suggested Miss Linton. 'We've got to come back through Armiford anyhow, so we can drop them at the end of the road. We can just squeeze them in.'

'Oh, would you take them?' asked Mrs Lucy. 'I'll be awfully glad if you can, for John has to visit the dentist this afternoon; and while Javotte can see to Barney and Vi, the other beauties are beyond her now. So it really would be a relief. Tell me what time you're coming back, and I'll meet them.'

Miss Burnett considered. 'The show should be over about 4.45; then tea in the café. Can you be at the end of the road by six?'

'Splendid! All right, then; you can go, you two!'

'Whoops!' shouted Betsy. 'Mummy, you're a duck of an angel, and I love you!'

'You'd better say all that to Miss Burnett and Miss Linton,' suggested her mother wickedly, knowing very well that Miss Betsy would never dare to do such a thing.

Eleven-year-old Julie regarded her younger sister with scorn. 'You are a little goop!' she said.

'I know someone who can easily be goopier—if there is such a word—when she tries,' said their mother swiftly. 'By the way, you two, mind you do as you're told. No silly tricks! That's a forbid, remember.'

'All right. We'll be good,' said Julie. 'Go on, Betsy! Promise Mummy you'll be good.'

'I promise,' repeated Betsy. And there is no doubt that they fully intended to keep their word.

Then Miss Burnett, remarking that they had better get off if they wanted to be in time, sent them all to don outdoor things, and presently they were walking two and two down the road. The cinema lay in the main shopping centre of the city, so they had to be circumspect. They were in plenty of time, and were shown to seats in the very front of the balcony. The nine small folk sat together, with Miss Linton at the far end, and the triumvirate next to Betsy Lucy at the other side. The prefects, elder girls, and

Miss Burnett were behind. There were not a great many people upstairs, though the auditorium was fairly full. The 'big' picture was all they could ask, being the tale of England in the time of the Napoleonic wars. The hero was a dashing young officer, while Eunice Brownlow proved to be as lovely as her picture, and a very good actress into the bargain. One exciting episode in which the young officer was accused of spying for the French and threatened with death at the hands of the infuriated mob, only to be saved by the courage of his betrothed, made the girls hold their breath. But all ended well with a final 'close-up' of the pair walking along the wild shore of 'Tedder's Cove' by moonlight, and finishing appropriately in each other's arms.

It was quite a shock to see the doors of the cinema swing open and the lights go up. They stumbled forth from the balcony to make their way to the café, which was situated on the ground floor. It was the unwonted excitement which made Betsy Lucy, an inveterate cat-lover, suddenly cry, 'Oh, look! What a lovely pussy!' and make a dive after the cinema's cat, a lordly Persian person of dark amber stripes on a buff background, who was sitting on the stairs.

At any rate, the little girl dashed forward, heedless of Miss Linton's imperative, 'Betsy! Keep with the others!' She missed her footing, and would have fallen down the stairs to the floor far below, had not Dorcas seen her in time, sprung forward, and grabbed her. Betsy, shoved against the railings by the elder girl's arm, clutched at them, and saved herself. Dorcas, overbalanced with the force of that push, slipped, tried to catch at the railings, and then crashed right to the bottom of the steps, where she lay, a pitiful little heap, just as the waiting queue for the downstairs seats was beginning to move in.

There was a chorus of shrieks from the girls, and another from the women in the queue. Almost at once a crowd gathered round

She crashed right to the bottom of the stairs.

her, and the commissionaire, summoned urgently by one of the box-office girls, had his work cut out to force his way through the throng. Miss Burnett, leaving the girls to Miss Linton, tore down the stairs. The manager emerged from his office, turned back with a sharp word of command to a couple of men behind him, and snatched his telephone receiver from its rest.

Then Miss Linton, pulling herself together, took Betsy in her arms, and bade the other girls follow her to the café in such a tone that they went without a murmur, where they were fully occupied in comforting the poor little cause of the accident. As for Miss Burnett, she had managed to fight her way through the crowd to where Dorcas lay, very still and white, while people all round made various suggestions as to what to do.

Some of them were for lifting her, and carrying her to one of the big settees that stood in the vestibule, but Mary Burnett sharply refused anything of the kind, and the commissionaire, an old R.A.M.C. man, backed her up.

'The boss'll have rung up the Ambulance Station,' he said. 'We'll leave 'er till the men come.'

Then his colleague appeared to hurry people into the cinema, and in a few minutes the seats were filled, and the great doors closed till there should be more vacancies. The commissionaire had produced a rug to cover Dorcas by this time, but he agreed with Miss Burnett that it was wisest to leave her alone. Unfortunately there had been no doctor in the place, though the manager had had a message asking for one flashed on the screen.

It seemed a never-ending period to Miss Burnett before there came a sharp rapping on the glass of the doors, and the ambulance men appeared, accompanied by a doctor who had been down at the station when the call came through. They brought their stretcher and stood quietly to one side while the doctor made a swift examination. Dorcas remained unconscious, but she moaned when he moved her, thus relieving the mistress's heart from a big burden. She had moved out of the way when he came, but still remained kneeling.

Presently he looked at her. 'Your kiddy?' he asked.

'One of our girls,' said Miss Burnett, speaking with stiff lips. 'We are from the Chalet School. Is she badly hurt?'

He shook his head. 'Don't know yet. She's broken her collar-bone and got a nasty bang on the head. I'll get her to the hospital and we'll see then. I hope not, but it's impossible to say at present.' He beckoned to the men, who lifted Dorcas on to the stretcher. She moaned again, but her eyes still remained closed.

The doctor looked at the mistress. 'Don't be frightened,' he said gently. 'Probably it's only the collar-bone and concussion. Where is the rest of your crowd?'

'My colleague would take them to the café. We were to have tea there,' said Miss Burnett.

'One of our girls,' said Miss Burnett.

'I see. Well, suppose you go and tell them what I have told you, and have your tea. Yes, I know you don't feel as if you could take anything, but you must try. Then, if she can take the other girls back to the school, you could come along to the hospital, and then we could tell you more definitely.'

Mary nodded. 'I must let Miss Linton know, anyhow.' Then she added, 'You—you'll let me see her, won't you?'

'Depends on the hospital authorities. But I don't suppose they will refuse you a peep, anyhow. What about letting her people know?'

'No use. They're in America. In any case, it will be better to wait till I have something definite to send. But I must get on to the Head and Matron and tell them. They're away. It's half-term.'

'Far away?'

'Oh, no; near Chepstow. They're on the 'phone, so I can ring them as soon as I know.'

'Very well. Now I must go. I'll see you later on.'

With that he departed, and Mary, after a few words with the manager, went to the café, where she found Miss Linton and the girls seated at two long tables in a quiet corner. A sumptuous tea had been spread, but the plates were very little depleted. The mistress set herself to cheer the girls, whose frightened faces showed how upset they were.

'You shouldn't have waited tea for me!' she said in tones as near her ordinary ones as she could manage. 'They've taken Dorcas to the hospital to set a broken collar-bone, and I expect they will keep her there for the next two or three days. Thank you, Miss Linton. I should like a cup of tea.'

Miss Linton poured it out, the colour coming back to her face. The girls, feeling reassured—Dorcas couldn't be very badly hurt, or Miss Burnett would never have asked for tea almost the first thing—fell to, and made quite a good meal. There was one exception. Gillian Culver gave Miss Burnett one quick glance, and then turned her attention to the cake she had on her plate, though she crumbled more than she ate.

As for Miss Linton, she said no more, but managed to swallow tea, bread-and-butter, and cake, just as Miss Burnett at the other table was doing. Betsy had recovered from her weeping fit, but she was red-eyed and very subdued between Gay and Clare, who plied her with cakes in a reckless fashion. Once the meal was ended, they left more or less thankfully. Miss Linton undertook to see the two Lucys safely into their mother's hands, and Miss Burnett set off to the hospital. She was met with the news that Dorcas was beginning to come round, and although she was bruised and cut, in addition to the broken bone and the huge lump on her head, there was said to be no fear of internal injuries.

The mistress was taken up to the ward, where she was permitted to look at her pupil, who had lost the greyish tinge she had had at first, and seemed considerably more like herself. Her head was bandaged, and her arm was in a sling, but apart from that, there was nothing to see. Mary Burnett sent up an unspoken thanksgiving to Heaven as she heard the nurse's reassuring remarks. Then, knowing that there was nothing more she could do, she withdrew, to be met by the doctor outside.

'Well, it's better than it might have been,' he said cheerily. 'And now, Matron says you can use her 'phone and let your Head know, if you think you ought. Come along, and I'll show you where her room is.'

He led the way, chatting cheerfully. When they reached Matron's room, he rang the Chepstow number, and then left her while she broke the news to Miss Wilson. When she came out, thankful that 'that' was over, and Bill had announced her intention of getting back to school as early as possible next day, she found him still there, waiting to run her out to Plas Howell in his car. She was therefore not very much behind the others in arriving, and was able to relieve everyone's mind by informing them that Dorcas was not seriously injured, and would soon be back at school again.

'What about America?' asked Miss Linton later on in the privacy of the Staff-room.

'Bill says she'll see to it. I'm thankful for that.'

'Think they're likely to come? And do sit down, Mary! You're ramping about like a caged tiger!'

Miss Burnett came and sat down. 'I *feel* restless. I can't tell you, Gill, how glad I am it's no worse. When I think—'

'Don't be silly. It wasn't your fault. Mrs Lucy said I was to be sure to tell you that. Also I was to say that she ought to have known better than to let you have Julie and Betsy, because if there *was* a chance of getting into mischief, her children seemed bound to take it, and they were as bad as Jo Maynard had ever been.'

Miss Burnett laughed for the first time since the accident. 'Impossible!' she said with finality. Then she added, 'I've no idea if the Browns will come or not, but I've solved *one* mystery today, Gillian. Dorcas Brown and Eunice Brownlow are sisters. Of that I'm convinced. Dorcas is simply a plain version of Eunice Brownlow. But why has the little donkey kept it so dark?'

'Ask me something I can answer,' replied Miss Linton, as she produced a box of sweets. 'Have one of these, and let's forget for half an hour that we are responsible members of this school.'

The conscientious Miss Burnett was so overcome by the exciting happenings of that day that she actually did as she was asked.

## Chapter V

### 'WE KNOW SOMETHING!'

B ill, I feel *awful* about it! And yet I don't see how I could have helped it happening.'

Miss Wilson, acting-Head of the Chalet School, leant back in her chair and surveyed her junior thoughtfully. 'I don't either. No matter who had been with the children, I imagine the same thing would have happened. Betsy Lucy is cat-mad, and she would make a dive for any member of the tribe she saw. And as Dorcas seems to have been nearest her at the time, it was to be expected that she would try to save the child from falling. Instead of suffering from a bad attack of enlarged conscience, Mary, just you be thankful it was Dorcas Brown, a sturdy, healthy girl, who had the accident. I got on to Matron this morning, and she tells me Dorcas is doing as well as possible. The concussion has quite passed off, and though she is sore and aching with her bruises and broken clavicle, she will soon be over that, and then it is just a question of the bone setting.'

'I'm glad to hear that,' said Miss Burnett fervently. 'What about letting her folk know?'

'I've written them by Air-mail. I waited till I got the hospital report. We shall probably hear from them in due course.'

'Do you think any of them will come?' asked Miss Linton.

'Doubtful. They are right away at Santa Barbara—at least, that's the address I have. As there is no danger, I doubt very much if they will come all that distance.'

'Bill!' said Miss Linton suddenly. 'We've solved a mystery, anyhow.'

'We've solved a mystery, anyhow,' said Miss Linton.

Miss Wilson stared at her. 'Solved a mystery? What are you talking about? *What* mystery have you solved?'

'Dorcas Brown's identity. She's a sister of Eunice Brownlow, isn't she?'

'I wondered if that film would give her away. Yes, she is. Her real name is Dorcas Brownlow.'

'Then why on earth is she here as "Dorcas Brown"?' demanded Miss Linton.

'Her mother arranged that. She saw Madame, and it was all fixed up when I was away with my cousin. I knew about her, of course, but I have no idea why she's dropped the end of her name. Do you think the girls have guessed?'

'Not so far as I know. The younger ones certainly won't—especially since she's cut herself a fringe.'

'She's—*what*?' demanded Miss Wilson.

'Oh, I forgot. You wouldn't know. Yesterday morning, Miss

Dorcas descended with a fringe, or, rather, Clare Danvers fetched her along to my room to exhibit it before breakfast. I got no sense out of her on the subject, so I left it for you to deal with. Of course, I see the reason now. She was afraid that if she went with her hair parted at one side someone would see and announce the likeness. She must have cut her hair to prevent it.'

'The imp!' Miss Wilson was laughing. 'Well, we can't very well deal with it now. I gather they've had to cut the hair away at one side of her head. She had a nasty gash, and they've had to put a couple of stitches in. If the girls haven't already noticed the likeness, I doubt very much if they'll see it now. Matron said they took about half her fringe away, as well as some of the long hair.'

'Poor child!' said Gillian Linton. 'She *will* look a little fright till it grows again!'

'Oh, we'll have to contrive some mode of hairdressing for her that will disguise it,' said Miss Wilson easily.

'But why on earth should she try to hide her relationship with Eunice Brownlow?' asked Mary Burnett. 'I should have thought she would have been proud of it. It's rather the sort of thing a good many girls would have boasted about.'

'I don't know. Perhaps her parents don't wish it to be known at present. Well, if you folk are going to take those girls for a walk before lunch, you'd better get on with it. It's half-past eleven now.'

'Is it so late? I'd no idea! Come on, Gill! We'd better send them to get ready.' Miss Burnett got up from her lowly seat on a pouffe as she spoke, and Miss Linton uncurled herself and left the corner of the big settee. Miss Wilson looked at them both, a warm affection in her grey eyes. She had known the pair from their early teens, when they had been pupils of the school. Miss Burnett was now twenty-eight, and Miss Linton was twenty-four, and that meant a good number of years of friendship between them.

'We've had worse things happen in this school,' she said. 'Dorcas is not seriously hurt, so take that anxious look off your face, Mary. Jo, for instance, has given us a good many greater trials than this. And you may remember how we used to worry over Robin Humphries. No one ever thought she would be even as strong as she is now. As I said before, Dorcas is sturdy, and she isn't the finely strung type that feels everything badly, as Jo is. Off you both go, and come back looking more like yourselves!'

They laughed, and left the room to summon their flock, and no more was said at the time. They all had a delightful walk, right up to the top of the hill, half-way up which Plas Howell was situated.

By four o'clock the rest of the school had begun to arrive, and once the girls had been told about the half-term happenings, things settled down to normal, and the school returned to its usual programme of hard work and thorough play. In addition, they had the Christmas play to prepare, so time was fully occupied.

Dorcas returned to school three weeks later, having been to stay with an aunt in Kent for a few days. She looked very much herself, for they had parted her hair in the middle, and clipped it back at each side. She had pulled forward a strand to cover the fresh scar, and then tied a snood round.

The girls welcomed her warmly, especially her own form, and she found, rather to her surprise, that she was almost a heroine. It was a trial to her in some ways, but she had to put up with it.

'Does your head hurt very much, Dorcas?' asked Frances Gray when she first saw her.

'Not now, but I had a ghastly headache for nearly a week,' said Dorcas with a slight shudder.

'Didn't you feel awful when you were falling?' asked someone else.

'Wouldn't you?' demanded Dorcas. 'For goodness' sake stop talking about it! I want to forget it if I can.'

'So I should imagine,' said Gay. 'No one is to mention it to Dorcas again. Do you hear, all of you? If anyone does, I'll report her to Matey. Come on, Dorks; let's go and do a spot of trig. for Miss Slater. You shall help me!'

Dorcas laughed, though she had felt like objecting to the unlovely abbreviation of her name. She realised that Gay had seen her discomfort and was trying to protect her, so she went off quite cheerfully, and the excitement gradually died down.

'You've got a part in the play,' said Jacynth later on in the week. 'Have you had it given you yet?'

'Yes, Gillian brought it this morning. Very short, thank goodness!'

Jacynth glanced at her curiously. It seemed a funny thing for a girl related to Eunice Brownlow to say. She said nothing, however, and Dorcas imagined fondly that her secret was a secret still.

'I wish Jo would hurry up and come back home,' said Gay, who was scribbling at her French in a wild attempt to get it finished before Mlle should arrive. They were in their form-room at the time. 'She's been away a fortnight now.'

'She'll be back next week,' remarked Peggy Burnett. 'Daisy Venables told Kitty so yesterday. Miss Wychcote's wedding takes place in three weeks' time, and she's to be married from Plas Gwyn, so Jo will have to get back for that.'

Gay frowned severely over her effort to translate 'There was a large number of people in the library yesterday, so I expect all the new books will have been borrowed' into French that was likely to satisfy Mlle. Then she looked up. 'What d'you think of the new play?'

'Finished, Gay?' asked Marie Varick. 'Isn't it a horrible exercise? As for the play, I think it'll be rather lovely when we get really going.'

'It's a good thing we've got a decent fiddler in the school,' observed Jacynth.

'And a very good thing we've a good selection of clothes!'

'Yes, hasn't Jo given us a wholesale collection of periods this time?' said Roosje Lange.

'I've only got my own part,' said Dorcas. 'What is the story of it?'

'Half a sec!' Gay scribbled industriously for a moment. Then she thumped her blotting-paper down on the exercise, capped her pen, and heaved a sigh of relief. '*That's* done, thank goodness! I call it wanton cruelty to set such an exercise for *any* girl! What is the time, anyone?'

'Five to eleven,' said Frances, looking at her watch. 'Goodness! What's happened to Mlle?'

'She's coming now,' said Marie Varick from her post near the open door. 'I can hear her heels.'

With one accord the Lower Fifth flung itself into its various places, and when little Mlle Lachenais arrived, it was to a roomful of the demurest damsels possible. She apologised for being late, and then set to work as if determined to make up for lost time. Lower Fifth that morning were catechised about rules of French grammar within an inch of their lives. In fact, as Jacynth said later, they hadn't a moment in which to draw a full breath until she left them.

'Whatever has happened to Mlle?' gasped Barbara Henschell as she sat back, fanning herself with her blotting-paper. 'I cannot remember such a lesson from her before. Bill—yes; also Miss Slater when she's on the warpath; but *Mlle*!'

'She simply hounded us,' said Gay, regarding her red-inked

exercise ruefully. 'I loathe having questions shot at me. My brain goes all fuzzy and I can't remember a thing.'

'Nor can I,' agreed Frances Gray.

'Why are you people chattering?' demanded a chilly voice from the doorway. 'What is your next lesson?'

The Lower Fifth rose to its feet as Miss Burnett entered the room. She was on her way to Upper Third, but, hearing the voices, had come to find out why Lower Fifth were not working. It was well past the beginning of the new lesson, as Mlle had kept them beyond the time.

'It's prep., Miss Burnett,' said Jacynth. 'Mlle has just left us.'

'I see. Well, will you please begin your preparation at once. Surely girls as old as you can be trusted to work for half an hour by yourselves? Don't let me hear any noise from you, or I must send to Miss Wilson to ask if someone can come and sit with you.' With this the history mistress withdrew, leaving a badly squashed

'She's coming now,' said Marie Varick.

Lower Fifth to take out its books and meekly devote the rest of the time to work.

Once the bell rang for the end of morning school however, and they were free to talk as they chose, they had plenty to say.

'What on earth has got into the Staff?' demanded Gay crossly. 'Mlle nearly works us off our heads; Miss Burnett is as squashing as a—a *tank*; and even Mrs Redmond was fussy over lit. There's something up!'

'Perhaps some of the babes are starting an epidemic!' suggested Frances. 'We had German measles last term. It may be mumps or chicken-pox now. That would upset them all right.'

'Everyone seemed to be at Prayers so far as I know,' said Barbara. 'What about your crowd, Marie?'

A Catholic, Marie Varick attended Prayers in the Kindergarten, being, with Roosje Lange, the only girl in Lower Fifth to do so. She thought hard for a minute or two.

'I think they were all there,' she said finally. 'Weren't they, Roosje? I didn't notice anyone away, anyhow.'

'Only Irene Williams,' said Roosje, 'and she's been down all the week with a bronchial cold. She's getting on all right, I know, for I saw Daphne before Prayers, and asked her, so it can't be her.'

'Then I give it up,' said Barbara.

However, they were soon to know what was wrong. When the gong sounded for dinner, they marched into the big dining-room as usual, and found themselves sitting down to a meal of boiled eggs, bread-and-butter, grated cheese, salad, all topped off with stewed gooseberries, which they recognised as some of their own bottling.

'I'm very sorry, girls,' said Miss Wilson after she had said Grace. 'There has been a chapter of accidents in the kitchen, and the dinner was completely ruined. As most of this happened about eleven, there was next to no time to arrange for anything better than this. We hope, however, to make up for it at supper-time.'

'Wonder what's happened!' mused Gay as she ate her egg. 'Has the ceiling fallen and smashed up everything?'

After dinner she voiced this idea to the rest.

'There might have been a fall of soot and a fire in the kitchen,' rejoined Jacynth.

'And *I* thought perhaps Cook had gone mad and chased all the others round the kitchen with the meat-chopper or the carving-knife,' confessed Marie Varick, whose tastes tended towards the blood-thirsty.

The Lower Fifth shrieked at this, and brought Miss Wilson on themselves. She laughed when she heard Marie's idea, but she rebuked them for making so much noise.

'You aren't babies now,' she said. 'Before many months are up, most of you will be Upper Fifth, I hope. You'd better begin to behave like it, hadn't you?'

The girls looked conscience-stricken, so she left them, and they settled down to their after-dinner rest.

It was not till tea-time that any of the girls knew what had happened. Then they heard the full story from Gillian, who had been talking with Jesanne Gellibrand. Far from chasing anyone round the kitchen, Cook had tripped over something on the floor just as she was removing a large frying-pan full of fat from the kitchen Aga. She had fallen headlong, burning herself badly on the Aga, and the pan had deposited its entire contents through an open vent on to the fire, which flared up. Cook's apron had caught, and she had only been saved by Gwladys, one of the maids, who had rushed forward with a large bowl of water in which she was washing cabbage, and flung the entire contents over her. The chimney had caught fire, and the whole dinner had been covered with soot, while the kitchen-maid, rushing to the rescue, likewise tripped, and caught at the first thing handy.

She flung the entire contents over her.

This happened to be a tray of plates ready to go into the big rack for heating, and the whole lot came down with a crash on to the tiled floor. What with a spoilt dinner, Cook *hors de combat*, and a shortage of plates—fifty-nine of them were in bits and a good many more were cracked and chipped—it had been impossible to provide the usual midday meal.

Talking it over afterwards with Jacynth and Dorcas, Gay declared that she would have given a good deal to have been in the kitchen when it all happened.

'It must have been a complete scream,' she said with a chuckle.

'What a flick it would make!' exclaimed Dorcas. Then she stopped short and turned slowly red.

Gay and Jacynth exchanged looks. Then Gay took the matter into her own hands. 'Look here, Dorcas, I think you'd better know that we—I mean Jacynth and Gillian and I—know why you won't talk about your homefolks like the rest of us. You're some sort of relation to Eunice Brownlow—sister, for choice. That's true, isn't it?' Then, as Dorcas dumbly nodded, 'Well, what we simply can't understand is why on earth you should want to keep it dark.'

She paused, but Dorcas remained dumb. Jacynth took up the story. 'If it were us, we'd be most fearfully proud. She's simply lovely, and a jolly good actress. Why on earth don't you want us to know? Why are you called Dorcas Brown when you're really Dorcas Brownlow? Surely you—you don't *mind*?'

Dorcas glanced round. They were in a little room where they had been sent to get on with their raffia-work, and there was no one else about.

'How many besides you two and Gillian know?' she asked.

'No one, I should think,' said Gay. 'Unless some of the prees do,' she added doubtfully.

'I don't believe they do,' said Jacynth. 'No one has ever said anything about it, and they'd be almost sure to have if they did.'

Dorcas knew what she meant well enough, though Mrs Redmond, the present English mistress, would have exclaimed with horror at the appalling mixture of personal pronouns. She thought hard for a minute. Then she made up her mind.

'All right. I'll tell you,' she said. 'When you've heard it all, you'll see just why I didn't want it to be known. But don't even *begin* to think I'm ashamed of Eunice. I'm not! I'm proud of her, awfully proud! And that's just one of the worst parts of it all!'

## Chapter VI

### Dorcas's Story

Before this promising beginning the importance of handwork faded into the background. Jacynth and Gay simply dropped the baskets they were supposed to be making, and gave their entire attention to Dorcas, who told them her tale then and there.

'We lived in England till I was six, and then Dad had to go to America on business. As he was to be away for ages, about nine or ten months, he decided to take us—Mummy, Eunice, and me—with him. Eunice was fourteen then. She's eight years older than I.'

'Was she as lovely then as she is now?' asked Gay eagerly.

'Oh, yes. She always was a picture. You couldn't see her properly in the flick because it isn't coloured, but she has dark brown hair with golden gleams in it, and her eyes are just the colour of forget-me-nots, and she has the loveliest complexion. And my sister who died was like her, only fairer.'

'Had you another sister?' asked Jacynth.

Dorcas nodded: 'Yes: Irene. She was two years younger than Eunice. She died when she was ten, and that's why Dad was going to take us with him. Mummy had fretted horribly about Irene, and though she did try to be brave, she couldn't manage it, and had an illness. Then the doctor said she ought to have a holiday when she got better, and this job came along, and Dad thought America *would* be a real change, so he took us.

'I remember the journey. It was an awful voyage crossing the Atlantic, for we had to sail in October. Mummy and I were both sick all the time, but Dad and Eunice weren't. The stewardess wouldn't let them have much to do with us. Mummy was really horribly ill. I wasn't so bad as long as I lay flat, but if I sat up, or tried to stand, I was sick at once. It was supposed to be a five days' trip, but we were two days overdue, so we were a whole week on the boat.

'There were lots of people, of course, and they took heaps of notice of Eunice because she was so pretty. She had such pretty ways, too. I mean, if an old lady wanted some wool held to be wound, Eunice would offer to hold it. She used to go to play every morning with two little boys whose mother was too ill to look after them. Dad has always been proud of her, and he loved hearing all the nice things people said about her. Mummy did too, when she was able to listen.

'There was a big man crossing too, and he took more notice of Eunice than almost anyone. He used to go for deck-prowls with Dad, and he arranged for them to sit at his table. When they had a party, he gave Eunice all his favours, and danced with almost no one else, although she was only a kid and there were lots of grown-up girls there. It made Dad prouder of her than ever.'

'I should jolly well think so!' interjected Gay. 'But did your father *let* her go to the dance? I mean, I know my people wouldn't have let *me*.'

'Well, he couldn't do anything else,' said Dorcas. 'Mummy wasn't able to look after her, you see. He couldn't take her into the smoking-room, for instance. Mummy said just what your people would have said when she heard of it. It was only for a week however, and it didn't hurt her. She was just as sweet and nice as ever.

'Well, when we got to America, the big man gave Dad his card. He was Harold Carlton, the film producer. And what's more, he said that if Dad and Mummy would agree, he'd like them to go out to Beverly Hills for a visit when Dad's business was done, and bring Eunice and me. He hadn't ever seen me, of course. He thought I was like Eunice.'

'So you are!' interrupted Jacynth. 'It's awfully funny how exactly like her you are.'

'An *ugly* likeness!' said Dorcas bitterly. 'I know all about it, thank you!'

'Rot!' said Gay tersely. 'You aren't ugly. Don't flatter yourself that way, my dear!'

Dorcas laughed with a somewhat forlorn laugh. 'Well, not ugly perhaps. It might almost have been better if I had been. I'm just ordinary. Eunice—well, you saw her for yourselves.'

'Madame says,' began Gay with reference to Lady Russell, the owner of the Chalet School, 'that we're given the face God meant us to have. He gives us the features and the colours and so on, but only we ourselves can make it ugly or beautiful, because it's what we *are* that settles that.'

'That doesn't go in the flicks,' returned Dorcas abruptly.

Gay had no more to say, so she fell silent, and Dorcas went on with her story.

'Dad thanked Mr Carlton, of course, but he didn't think any more about it. His work took him to Boston, where we got a kind of flat. Eunice and I went to school, and no one ever thought we'd get any further west than that. But Dad found, however, that he'd have to go to St Louis, and he didn't like leaving Mummy and us alone, especially as Mummy was still not awfully strong. He took us, and then he had to go on again to California. Just then he remembered Mr Carlton's card, and wrote to him. A letter came back inviting all four of us to stay at his house for a month or two.

'I remember how Dad laughed and said that Americans were the most hospitable folk he'd ever known. Mummy wasn't too anxious to go; but she hadn't got on as we'd hoped, and when Dad asked her doctor in St Louis, he said it would be just the thing, so we went. Mr Carlton met us, though I didn't know anything about it, because we didn't arrive till after midnight, and I was fast asleep in Dad's arms. It was eighteen months since the voyage, for when Dad had finished one job, he'd done it so well, his firm sent him on another—that was the St Louis business. Then they sent him to California after that. I was nearly eight, and Eunice was just sixteen.

'There'd been a class for ballet dancing at our school, which Eunice had attended. She loved it, and did wonderfully. I don't mean she could have been a ballerina or anything like that. She'd begun too late, of course, but she did really well. When we moved on to St Louis, there was another class there, which she joined. I learned, too, but I was never so fond of it as she, and I didn't make the same progress. You see, she is naturally graceful, and I am not!

'Being in America had somehow made her quite grown-up. I was much younger and not really a companion for her. She used to call me "Baby," and pet me almost as if she was my mother—well, say, my aunt, and I felt rather that way too.

'When we saw Mr Carlton again, he whistled as he saw Eunice. Then he looked at me, and—oh, I can't tell you what it was like. His face changed, and he stared, first at her, and then at me. He said to Dad: "Well! What a difference!" I knew what he meant all right, even though Dad pretended to think he was referring to her being nearly grown-up, and my being just a kiddy.

'A week later he talked very seriously to Dad and Mummy. He wanted Eunice for a flick. There was what he called a "sub-deb part" in one he was just going to make, and they couldn't get the right girl for it. They'd tried out two or three, but none of them would do. Now Eunice had come along, and she had everything he wanted—looks, beautiful carriage, and a lovely voice. The part was that of an English girl, and even though we'd been to school with American girls, Mummy had taken care not to let us talk like them. He made Eunice the most wonderful offer, and promised that she should be looked after if Dad had to go home and wanted to take us with him.'

'But—she was still at school!' protested Jacynth.

'Yes, but she wouldn't have stayed more than another year anyhow. However, Mummy and Dad wouldn't agree at first. Mummy said it wasn't at all the sort of life she wanted for one of her girls; Mr Carlton raised his offer; he got hold of Eunice, and told her all the wonderful things that would happen, how she would be the second "World's Sweetheart," and how she'd have piles of money by the time she was twenty-five, and be able to do anything she liked. Then she begged Mummy and Dad to let her do it. They wouldn't at first, and then—well, then she went queer. She wouldn't sit with us, and she wouldn't play with me. She would scarcely kiss us, and once I overheard her say to Mummy, "You're spoiling my life for your stupid, old-fashioned ideas! Well, I can tell you this! You can make me do what you say now, I suppose, but when I'm twenty-one, I'll be my own mistress, and I'll come straight here and go into the flicks."

'Oh, it was a dreadful time, though I didn't know so much of it as I do now. I was too little; they'd got a French governess for me, and I was with her most of the day. It ended as you know. They gave in. Mummy said she'd lost one girl, and she couldn't bear to lose another. Daddy's firm had made him an offer to represent it in America for the next five years. We could make our home in California, and he would come back when he wasn't travelling. Mummy made one condition, and both Eunice and Mr Carlton had to agree to it. Whenever Eunice was on the set, Mummy was to be there too. She was to come straight home when she had finished working. They both tried to talk her out of it, but she stuck to it, and said if they wouldn't agree we'd all go home at once. So they agreed.

'Mr Carlton found a house with a lovely garden for us, and Maddy came too, so that my lessons could go on. Besides, they had to have someone to look after me, as Mummy and Eunice would often be out all day. Daddy took the post, and it was all settled. Eunice insisted on sending me to dancing-school, and doing all sorts of things of that kind. She kept saying that when I grew older I'd improve. Only, I never have done.'

She paused, but Gay and Jacynth had nothing to say. As Gay told Gillian later on: 'There just wasn't anything *to* say. I'd never met anything like it before.'

Dorcas continued: 'Eunice got the part, and a jolly good contract for the next five years. She did really well, though it was only a small part and she hadn't a lot to do. All the critics noticed her, and said she was worth watching. She had to work

'I'll come straight here and go into the flicks.'

frightfully hard, and she has told me since that more than once she nearly "jacked the whole thing up." She would have to do the same scene twenty or thirty times over just to get one tiny gesture exactly as the producer wanted it. Then whole chunks of what she had done were cut when they finished the shooting. However, she was a success all right, and she had minor parts in two or three other flicks. Besides that, California suited Mummy. She'd got fairly strong again, and then they found that she was quite a good actress herself, and began to use her, casting her for "mother" parts. She was awfully bucked to be able to earn, too. They played her and Eunice together in one picture, and it made a stir, even though Lamia Norog had the chief part.

'And then, two years later, Mummy suddenly said she wanted to come home, if it was only for a visit. Her contract was up, and Eunice's would be shortly. Mummy flatly refused to allow either of them to be tied up again till they'd had a year away from it, and I think Dad was pleased in one way. We sold our house in Beverly Hills, and came back. They sent me to boarding-school because Mummy wanted me to have an English education. She and Eunice went back to our old house, which the tenants had just left. Dad didn't come then; he couldn't. He followed about five months later. By that time we'd left our old home. Everyone knew about Eunice, of course, and she and Mummy said it was simply awful. There was plenty of money, for Mummy had made Eunice bank two-thirds of what she earned, and she'd done the same herself. She bought a lovely old house out in the country, with a high wall all around, and Mummy had huge iron gates put up that were kept locked most of the time, and they got a little peace that way.

'Mummy was glad to be finished, I think, but on Eunice's twenty-first birthday a most marvellous offer came to her, and she insisted on taking it. She signed the contract and sent it off, and then told Mummy and Dad what she'd done. That was two years ago. She sailed for California almost at once, and Mummy went with her, because she said I was safe at my school, and Daddy was in England, anyhow, and could look after me. She wasn't going to let Eunice go out there without her.

'Dad adores Mummy, and he got his firm to send him out again, and so they all are there at Santa Barbara now.'

'Well, but I don't see why all this should make you want to pretend you don't belong to them, and change your name and all that,' said Gay, looking at her with wide eyes.

'Oh, if it were only *that*!' cried Dorcas. 'Don't you see what happened? At my school—my last one, I mean—I was Dorcas Brownlow, of course, and everyone knew I was Eunice's sister. They used to come and ask me for stories about her. Some of the girls were awfully friendly to me, and I thought they liked me for myself, but they didn't. They hoped that when Eunice came back—she's coming in the spring—I would introduce them and take them home, and then they could swank about knowing the film star Eunice Brownlow. I only discovered it when I was out to tea with a cousin of Mummy's. She'd taken me to a café, and we were sitting in an alcove, and suddenly I heard the voice of the girl I'd thought was my best friend. She was saying, "Oh, she's quite a common little thing."

'I didn't understand, and I was just going to get up and go and tell her I was there and suggest that we have tea together, when I heard her mother say, "Then why are you so friendly with her?" She said, "Oh, Mums! How can you be so stupid? She's Eunice Brownlow's sister, of course. I mean to know Eunice Brownlow, and so I've been as decent as I could to Dorcas. Not that *she's* a bit like a film star. She isn't! She's downright plain, almost ugly. She can't act for toffee. Eunice Brownlow is simply lovely. You said so yourself when we went to see her in 'Cavalier's Daughter.'

I can't imagine how she and Dorcas come to be sisters! Of course, they're nobodies. Girls like that are generally the daughters of dustcart men, or coal-miners. Dorcas looks just like that! But you see, don't you, that I've *got* to keep in with her if I want to know Eunice."

'The waitress came just then, and they must have paid their bill and gone, for they weren't there when we left. I looked to see.'

'But—but didn't your cousin hear it?' cried Jacynth.

Dorcas shook her head. 'Cousin Theo was deaf, poor darling. She didn't hear anything unless you shrieked at her or she was using her electric thing, and she hadn't it going just then.'

'Well, I think that girl was an utter beast!' said Gay with decision. 'I hope you told her so.'

'Oh, I did! I was boiling mad. As soon as I got in, I found her, and I told her exactly what I thought of her. She tried to laugh it off, but I wouldn't let her. Then she got angry, and she said—oh, hateful things! I'm not going to repeat them. I want to forget them if I can.' Dorcas shuddered.

'*Don't* think of them!' ordered Gay. 'It's over and done with, but I'd like to get that girl into a quiet corner and tell her just exactly what she deserved!'

'What happened after that?' asked Jacynth.

'Oh, she knew she wouldn't get to know Eunice after that, so she just went ahead, and tried to turn all the girls against me. She did it, too. She was awfully clever, and a great favourite, and they listened to her. All the people I'd thought were my friends wouldn't have anything to do with me, and it got worse and worse. Then Eunice wrote to say Mummy was coming to England. She'd read a marvellous historical tale by a writer called Josephine M. Bettany, and they'd written to try and get the film rights, but the author wouldn't agree. Eunice said she would die if she couldn't make that picture, and so Mummy was coming personally to try to persuade the publisher to get her to agree. She came to see me, and wanted to know what was wrong. I couldn't tell her, of course. But I did say I hated the school and was miserable, and I begged her to take me away. So she did, and sent me here. I was determined not to have all that over again, so I got her to say my name was to be Dorcas Brown, and I hoped nobody would ever find out who I really was. Only you've done it, and what are you going to do about it?'

'Nothing, of course,' said Gay calmly. 'You must tell the girls yourself if you want them to know. 'Tisn't our business.'

Dorcas looked at her. 'Do you mean that?'

'Of course I do. And it goes for Jac and Gill, too.'

'And, anyhow, you needn't be afraid of that sort of thing here, Dorcas,' added Jacynth. 'We aren't howling snobs in *this* school, you know.'

Dorcas looked at them. She opened her lips to speak. Then

She sprang up from her chair, and rushed from the room.

she suddenly uttered a queer sound, half sob, half laugh, sprang up from her chair, and rushed from the room.

'Gone to cry somewhere,' said Gay shrewdly. 'Poor kid! What a time she seems to have had! Well, we must just try to make it up to her, but I'm glad to have solved *that* mystery, anyhow. Only we mustn't say a thing to her about it unless she begins.'

'No; she wouldn't like it,' agreed Jacynth soberly. Then she looked at her basket. 'What on earth will they say to us? We've done next to nothing, and we've been here an hour at least.'

'We've twenty minutes left,' said Gay practically. 'Come on; let's do what we can before the gong sounds for supper.'

## Chapter VII

### END OF TERM

The next excitement was Miss Wychcote's wedding. She was to be married from Plas Gwyn, with Dr Maynard to give her away, and Joey Maynard to 'act the heavy mother,' to quote herself. Jo's triplet daughters were to be bridesmaids, and the bridegroom was one of the doctors from the Sanatorium. Altogether the school felt that they might look on it as one of 'their' weddings.

They had had a collection, and presented the bride with a tea-service as the result, and an invitation had come for them. Miss Wilson had flatly refused to allow the whole school to go; she said that each form might send one representative, who was to be elected, and as the Chalet School contained eleven forms, that meant quite a party of them.

The voting duly took place, and eleven young ladies, headed by Jesanne Gellibrand, the head-girl, were seen off by an excited school on the morning of the December day which was to turn Phoebe Wychcote into Phoebe Peters. Lower Sixth was represented by Daisy Venables, Mrs Maynard's 'niece-by-marriage' as they called it; Gillian Culver had been chosen by Upper Fifth; and naturally Gay was the choice of Lower. They came back late in the afternoon, full of the ceremony. Miss Wychcote had made a charming bride, and the wedding luncheon had been a joy. Best of all, there came with them the second tier of the wedding-cake, so that everyone could taste it, and 'eat good luck to the bride,' to quote Gay.

The next week serious rehearsals for the Christmas play began and lessons were more or less in abeyance after eleven o'clock. Each year the school gave one of these plays, and only on two occasions had it been wanting. Lady Russell had written the first plays for them, but the previous year, Joey Maynard had been coaxed to 'try her hand.' She had done this year's, too, as her sister was too busy with the tiny daughter who had come in September. Carols were scattered throughout, so that, besides rehearsing the scenes, the players had extra singing; Mr Denny, singing-master at the school for more years than he cared to remember, trained them very carefully. There were solos, too, and the girls chosen had to practise hard, for Plato, as he was always called, was exigent to the last degree. Dorcas had a small part as an old woman, and Gay had been chosen for an archangel. As Jo had said, you couldn't waste that mop of golden curls which she possessed!

Gillian Culver was a young woman, and Jacynth Hardy was a musician, and had to play a short solo on her beloved 'cello. There were speaking parts for quite a large number of people, and the rest were dancers, mummers, and various other 'crowd' folk, the tiny Babies being baby angels.

For a whole fortnight the school talked play, thought play, and even, as some of them declared, *dreamt* play. Such lessons as were done were very sketchy, and various mistresses complained bitterly. However, as Miss Wilson said indulgently, it lasted for just a fortnight, after all. Next term, the girls must make it up. Then she told the united Staff a secret at which they cheered so lustily that the noise reached the girls and drove them nearly wild with curiosity to know what it meant, and there were no more complaints.

By common use the play was given on the last Saturday of term in the village hall, which was decorated by the girls on the

Friday night after they had finished their final rehearsal. In the morning they were not called till eight o'clock, and when they had had breakfast, they were set to checking up on library books, stock cupboard, chemistry apparatus, and various other odd jobs to keep them busy without tiring them too much. Dinner came at twelve, and then they all drove down to the village in the school buses, taking with them any clothes or 'props' that had been forgotten the day before.

Once in the dressing-rooms at the back of the hall proper, they were divided up among the mistresses who had undertaken to act as dressers. Two or three of the younger mistresses were to be on duty at the doors, and Miss Burnett had come down on her bicycle so as to be able to run any emergency errands that might crop up.

The play was to begin at half-past two, and by ten past, everyone was dressed and ready, and the hall was filling rapidly. Lady Russell and her husband, Sir James Russell, had already arrived with their two younger daughters—Josette, who would be a pupil at the school after the next summer, and Baby Ailie, who slumbered peacefully through it all. Several of the old girls who were married and living round about were also there, among them Joey Maynard's three closest friends, Frieda von Ahlen, Marie, Countess von und zu Wertheimer, and Madame de Bersac, once Simone Lecoutier, who, besides being an old girl, was also an old mistress. They had brought those of their families who were not already at the school—Marie's only girl was a member of the Kindergarten, and her son was in the Second Form. There was a goodly number of familiar and loved faces besides.

Gay Lambert, peeping through the curtains, announced to Jacynth standing behind her: 'Grandma and the Family are all there in the fifth row. See them, Jac?' and indicated a row where a stern-faced dame sat at one end, with a string of children and a pleasant-looking couple beside her.

'I wonder if she'll throw peppermints at us to "stay our stomachs"!' whispered Jacynth back with an involuntary giggle. 'I've never known her yet when she hadn't some handy.'

'Nor have I! Let's hope she doesn't *chuck* them at us, though!'

Then Nemesis descended on them in the shape of Miss Linton, who demanded to know what they thought they were doing, and drove them firmly back to the dressing-room.

Jo Maynard herself, coming in with the prompt copy of the play in her hand and a portentous frown on her brow, demanded to know if everyone was there.

'I hope so,' said Miss Linton doubtfully. 'Is it time, Jo?'

'Almost. I'm going over to "Prompt," anyhow. Do the men know the signals?' demanded Jo.

'Well, they've been rehearsed enough, goodness knows! Anyhow, we can't do any more about it now.'

'All right. I'll just take a look-see. Here, Dorcas!' seizing on the nearest person, 'you come with me, and I'll send you back with the message when we've called for lights down.' And gripping the French fishwife firmly by one wrist, and nearly causing her to drop her knitting, Joey steered through the excited groups of girls on to the stage, and applied her eye to the peephole.

Then she executed a brief but excited dance, much to Dorcas's surprise, and turned a pair of eyes glowing with joy on the girl. 'All serene! Trot back and tell them I'm going to call for house lights to be lowered, and ask Miss Slater to ring the bell for the orchestra.'

Dorcas padded back, nearly falling over her long skirt, and gave the message. The lights went down, a steady amber lime flooded

Joey steered through the excited groups of girls on to the stage.

the stage, and the people on for the opening took their places. The orchestra, duly warned, drifted into a low, sweet strain of music. Then the voices rose in the old English carol, 'Stars all brightly gleaming,' after which the curtains were swept back to reveal 'an old English hall.' A long table ran from back to front of the stage, and at one side was a magnificent log fire, with yellow paper flames leaping up round it, and a warm glow made by red electric bulbs cunningly hidden among the logs. At the two sides of the table was a motley crew, garbed in the attire of the Middle Ages, and at the head sat a lady and gentleman, Lois Bennett, the Games Prefect, and Meg Farrant, a quiet member of Lower Sixth. A magnificent butler was hurrying about with some attendants, serving the company.

Presently there came a cry of 'The boar's head! The boar's head!' and the butler hustled out, to return with a huge dish on which was placed a papier-maché boar's head, wreathed in ivy and holly, and really smoking! Miss Linton had arranged a bowl of boiling water beneath it, and there were slits through which the steam could come. The choir broke into the Boar's Head Carol as the butler circled round the stage, his trophy held high, before he set it on the side-table. Incidentally, as he came to the front of the stage, he started so violently that he nearly dropped his burden, and only recovered himself by a miracle. But no one noticed it. As he set the dish down, however, he muttered to his nearest attendant: 'Look over to the right. Third row!' which the attendant did, and nearly forgot to come in on his cue as a result. However, it passed off, and the next excitement was the entry of the mummers, who performed a delightful show, ending in a Yorkshire sword dance.

This was followed by the entry of the Yule log, dragged in by seven boys—Frances Coleman, Peggy Burnett, Marie Varick, and four people from Lower Fourth, with Wolferl Wertheimer riding in triumph on it. They signalised this by singing 'On Christmas Day in the Morning,' and then the curtains fell.

'Did you see?' gasped the butler, now safely off the stage. Some of the Junior mistresses were hurriedly removing the table, forms, and chairs, and dragging into place a cardboard arrangement to hide most of the 'fire.'

'See what?' demanded Lois Bennett.

'Miss Annersley's there—sitting at the side in a big chair!'

'*No!*' The noble lord made for the stage, but was promptly hauled back, and reminded where he was, by Miss Linton.

This was all the girls required to set them on the extreme tiptoe of excitement. Miss Annersley, the actual Head of the school, was loved only this side adoration by all her pupils, and her long absence had been bemoaned by them on many occasions. Miss Wilson was a dear, and they were all fond of her, but

Miss Annersley meant even more to them. Miss Wilson herself knew this and heartily concurred in it. Miss Annersley and she were close companions; she rejoiced in her friend's hold on the girls.

The next scene showed a Breton fisherman's cottage, and told how Christmas is celebrated on that rockbound coast. It began with the children waking in the morning to run to find their shoes and see what l'Enfant Jésu had left in them. Then they spoke of the glory of the music of the Christmas Mass, and the giving of alms to such poor as came that day. Dorcas, as the old grandmother, grumbling at the new ways when her granddaughters went off to a dance, made quite a hit. The carols in this scene were the Angevin 'Fésans Raijouissance' and the old Breton 'Dors, Saint Enfant,' this last being sung behind the scenes by Daisy Venables, who owned a soprano that gave promise of bringing her to concert work, so sweet and powerful was it.

The curtains fell again to rise on a Russian scene. Jesanne Gellibrand, as a young Russian woman, was keeping the holy feast according to the old ways told her by her aged grandfather in a log hut in the forest. Some of the Middles had badly wanted to introduce the howling of wolves to add a little more local colour, but this had been forbidden. Jesanne sang an English version of a Russian carol in a voice that was very true and sweet, if of small volume.

Then the curtains closed, and the Choir rendered 'Dans cet Etable' with great beauty of tone and diction. Silence fell after this; the curtains were lifted to one side, and Gay came forth in her flowing white robes, great wings made of buckram with paper 'feathers' soaring above her head, and a circlet of gilded buckram making an aureole on her curls. She stood for a moment with hand upraised for attention; then she spoke the first verse of the play:

'The night is still, the skies are dark,
 The winds are all asleep.
 The shepherds in the upland fold
 Keep watch beside their sheep.
 Only down in the city,
 In a shed where the cattle throng,
 The great beasts kneel, adoring
 A Babe and a Mother's song.'

On the last words Gabriel drew back, the curtains were raised, and the Manger Scene at Bethlehem was displayed to the hushed audience.

In the centre of the stage stood the crib, with the Bambino the school owned displayed in it. Over it, with eyes on the baby figure, leaned Daisy Venables as the Blessed Virgin, in a blue robe, her long white veil falling over her fair hair, and her face softened and sweet with the solemnity of the part. Behind stood the St Joseph, clad in green, holding a lantern. It had been impossible to introduce much in the way of animals, but the Maynards' big St Bernard, Rufus, lay at Daisy's feet, his chin on the edge of the crib, his eyes, too, on the image of the Christ Child lying with arms outstretched to embrace the whole world; and one of the near-by farmers owned a dainty little Alderney cow which was a family pet, and she stood at the other side, looking wonderingly at the scene before her.

For two minutes the audience feasted their eyes on the lovely picture. Its figures were lit by one amber beam; the rest of the stage was shadowy. Then the curtains closed, and Gabriel spoke again:

'The silence breaks. An angel song
 Rings to the list'ning earth.
 The sky is filled with golden light

And all with holy mirth.
Up spring the startled shepherds
To know what means this thing.
And their fears are stilled as the angels tell
Of the birth of the Baby King.'

Once more the curtains parted. This time the shepherds were standing, half crouching, or in the act of rising, crooks in their hands, shading their eyes to look up to the right where, on a staging, stood the group of the herald angels. At the back was another group playing on stringed instruments. There was silence while the tableau was shown. Then, as the curtains fell, came a great burst of song in Peter Warlock's arrangement of the old carol 'Tyrley, Tyrlow,' with the 'cello playing the part intended for the woodwind instruments between the verses.

When it ended, Gabriel spoke with increased solemnity:

'Then how they ran to Bethlehem
To offer Him their love!
How stilled when forth they came
From God, come from above!
And though great kings came fast and far
With royal gifts from the East,
Yet the Heart of the Holy Babe was warm
With the gifts of shepherd and beast.'

The picture this time was of the cave again. The shepherds knelt with their crooks, and the traditional Three Kings entered with their gifts of gold, frankincense, and myrrh. It was all aglow with light; round the sides and clustered in the corners were angels, all in snowy white, with wings, some tinted, some touched with gold, some as white as the flowing robes. Then the curtains fell, and Gabriel took up his story for the last time. His voice was full of gaiety as he spoke, for Jo had departed from the usual ending, and gave them the mirth and joyousness of Christmas in her play.

> 'Come forth, come forth, good Christians all!
> And greet our Baby King.
> Come from all corners of the world,
> And join us as we sing!
> Right merrily dance and gaily chant
> In a love-ring for very joy,
> For here is our Monarch come down to the earth,
> Our Jesus, the Holy Boy!'

Up went the curtains; all the actors crowded on the stage. The Madonna was holding up the Bambino, and a smile was on her face.

The angels had caught hands to form a ring round the humans, leaving only the front open, so that the grouping was visible to the audience. All held up gifts. It was a scene of the utmost gaiety. Then the orchestra broke into the gay old Burgundian carol, 'Patapan!', and they sang it, skipping round the group of the Holy Family, and singing with all their hearts.

When the curtains fell, most people thought that that was the end, but Jo had chosen to mark the contrast. The final tableau showed everyone kneeling, while the strains of the beautiful 'Adeste Fideles' filled the hall with a great swell of song, reminding everyone that, though Christmas brings merriment and joy, it also should mean worship.

The play ended on a grave note, but there was nothing grave about the crowd of girls that suddenly came pouring through the doors into the hall in search of one member of the audience. Miss Annersley, waiting till the village folk had got away, was

Miss Annersley was surrounded by a throng of laughing people.

surrounded by a throng of laughing people who all wanted to know how she was, and when she would be coming back to school.

'Not till the summer term at soonest,' she told them; and there was a loud groan. Then Miss Wilson, with an anxious eye to her friend's well-being, came to sweep her off to the school in a car, and the girls went back to change and clear up.

They were allowed to see their beloved Head once more before she went off in her car to the Russells' home, the Round House, where she was to spend the night, before going back to her temporary home near Chepstow.

'I hear you've been splendid while I've been away,' she said as she stood on the daïs in Hall, looking at them all. 'The doctors won't let me start work till after Easter; but if I go on as well as I'm doing now, I hope to be back with you then. A very happy Christmas to you all, new girls as well as old. God bless every one of you!'

She left after that, and the girls were set to dancing till bed-time. Half-way through the evening Dorcas contrived to get Gay and Jacynth into a corner.

'I didn't know a school could be like this,' she said. 'I was afraid after the last time, but now I see I was silly. I'm going to tell Miss Wilson and ask her to put me down as Dorcas Brownlow. I shall tell Mrs Maynard, too, and ask her if she won't change her mind about *The Leader of the Lost Cause*. I was going to try to do it behind her back, sort of, but now I know, I'm going to be quite straight about it. Eunice's contract with Mr Carlton is up in March, and she and Mummy are coming home, so perhaps they could make the picture here, and Mrs Maynard wouldn't mind that. You can tell the others who I am. Only do get it over, and let me start fair next term.'

'Right you are!' said Gay. 'We'll tell Gill, because she guessed first of all, you know, and then we'll let the rest of our form into the secret. It'll go all over the school after that.'

And so it did. By the end of term everyone knew that Dorcas Brown was really Dorcas Brownlow, and sister of 'that wonderful girl Eunice Brownlow,' as Mollie Avery said. Dorcas found that, though they were all thrilled, there was no self-seeking in their delight. When she said that Eunice would be sure to visit the school when she came back to England, Frances voiced the general feeling by saying: 'But are you sure it won't bore her, just coming to school? Of course we'd love it if she did,' she added hastily.

No one said anything to her about the reason for making such a mystery about her identity. Jesanne, Gillian, and one or two of the others had seen to that after hearing Gay's somewhat lurid account of how she had been treated at her other school. She had rather dreaded that part of it, but, thanks to the elders, it was taken quite naturally.

THE MYSTERY AT THE CHALET SCHOOL

'Goodbye, Dorks,' said Gay when they parted at the railway station on breaking-up day, Gay having to go on to King's Cross with a dozen or so other girls, and Dorcas being met by Cousin Theo, with whom she was to spend the holidays. 'Jolly glad you've come to the school. Have good hols!'

'I'm jolly glad, too,' said Dorcas, 'and I'm jolly glad not to be a mystery any more. It was very wearing!'

Then Cousin Theo arrived, and they parted, Gay going off laughing, with her arm through Jacynth's, and Dorcas, kissing Cousin Theo, glad to remember that, when next term came, she at least would not be the mystery at the Chalet School.

'As for Dorcas Brown, she's a plain mystery.'

With a laughing nod she went out, her arm round Daisy.

They flung themselves on the girl who stood in the doorway.

A mistress was waiting to escort them with a torch.

'Come up to my room,' said the Matron.

Dorcas pushed it aside. 'I'm sick of the stupid flick!' she burst out.

'Good gracious, Clare! What's wrong?'

She crashed right to the bottom of the stairs.

'One of our girls,' said Miss Burnett.

'We've solved a mystery, anyhow,' said Miss Linton.

'She's coming now,' said Marie Varick.

She flung the entire contents over her.

'I'll come straight here and go into the flicks.'

She sprang up from her chair, and rushed from the room.

Joey steered through the excited groups of girls on to the stage.

Miss Annersley was surrounded by a throng of laughing people.

# Robin Heeds the Call

BY

SHEENA WILKINSON and SUSANNE
BROWNLIE

# Robin Heeds the Call

Cars and buses splashed through the puddles on the Bethnal Green Road. The slight, dark-haired girl jumped back from the pavement and surveyed her soaked skirt.

'Bother,' she said, and a shadow fell briefly across her lovely face. But there was no time to waste.

Robin pulled her coat tighter around her, broke into a run, and ten minutes later turned into the dark alleyway where Frau Gradl had her room. 'At least, if I'm wet, I'm not exactly cold,' she thought, almost missing her footing on the slippery iron steps. She hesitated a moment at the doorway, heart pounding with dread, but she knew that she must face what lay ahead.

The dark little room was very stuffy, and Robin, even as she called a cheery 'Grüss Gott' to the child at Frau Gradl's bedside, struggled to push up the heavy sash.

It was clear that the woman was sinking fast. Robin took in the hectically flushed cheeks, the eyes bright with fever and the skeletal hands plucking at the grubby blanket.

'Frau Gradl?'

But the woman was beyond speech.

The child raised a tear-stained face to Robin. 'Mamma—kept calling for Papa,' she said, in an accent which suggested that English was not her mother-tongue. 'But now she—she does not speak.' Her brown eyes filled with tears.

In defiance of everything she knew was common sense, Robin bent over the dying woman. The laboured breathing quietened as Frau Gradl grasped Robin's hand with a surprisingly strong grip.

'Sabine?' she rasped.

'She's here,' Robin said shakily. 'And Sister Bernadette will be here any minute. She must be held up in the storm—that's why I took so long.'

Where was Sister Bernadette? Robin's months of settlement work in the East End of London had accustomed her to the misery of grinding poverty, but now she longed for the reassuring presence of the Irish nun. Robin had been working with the Gradls for some months, chosen because of her fluency in the German which was Frau Gradl's only language. She had always known that Frau Gradl was very frail, but she had not realised that the woman's hold on life was so precarious. As Sabine clasped her mother's thin hands, muttering endearments in rapid guttural German, Robin bit her lips and suppressed a shiver.

'Fräulein Humphries?' The child turned to Robin. 'Mamma will get well, will she not?'

'I—I—'

But Robin could find no words of consolation. It seemed to her that Frau Gradl could not possibly recover, but how could she tell this forlorn little girl that she was soon to be orphaned? In an attempt to comfort her, she drew Sabine to her. She tried again. 'Blümchen, your mamma is very ill. She has suffered a great deal. Perhaps—'

The nun's tread was so quiet that Robin heard nothing until Sister Bernadette was in the room. In one movement Sabine pulled away from Robin and buried her head in the young nun's breast.

'Mamma is going to the hospital now,' Sister Bernadette said in her soft Irish voice. She looked at Robin over the tousled little head. 'I telephoned for an ambulance on my way. I knew it would be needed,' she murmured, glancing at the woman in the bed. Frau Gradl seemed, to Robin's inexperienced eyes, to be sleeping peacefully but when Sister Bernadette lifted the thin wrist to take her pulse, the nun's face clouded.

'Now, Sabine, child.' She smiled reassuringly at the little girl. 'Remember that we're all in God's hands—he'll take care of your mammy, and he won't leave you either. I think we'll have a decade of the rosary while we wait.'

She pulled the beads from the pocket of her habit. Robin's rosary, a gift from her beloved adopted sister Jo, was at home in her digs, but the familiar words comforted her as nothing else could. She noticed how the nun could tell her beads with one hand, while stroking the damp hair back from Sabine's tearstained cheeks with the other.

Robin had always been struck by Sister Bernadette's calm competence in their work together, but never more so than now. Even Sabine, by the third Hail Mary, was repeating the words in her broken English.

'Why couldn't I have brought her this comfort?' Robin thought, stifling the cough that was starting to prickle at the back of her throat. As the prayers drew to a close, she gave in to it.

Sister Bernadette frowned. 'You need to get yourself home and out of those wet clothes,' she said. 'You don't need to worry about Sabine; there's a place for her at St Anne's while her mother is in hospital—and for as long she might need it.'

The child looked up in alarm, and Sister Bernadette continued in softer tones, 'And I'll be there to keep a special eye on her.'

Robin suppressed another cough. 'I wish I could do more. I should stay until the ambulance comes,' she protested, but Sister Bernadette hushed her.

'For goodness' sake, haven't you worn out your shoe leather coming to see them day in and day out? Now hurry on home and get into a hot bath.'

The firm kindness of the nun's admonishment reminded Robin

of Matron back at school, and she acquiesced, suddenly aware of how shivery she felt, and of the weight of her sodden coat and skirt. She kissed Sabine.

'I promise I'll come and visit you soon, Blümchen. The nuns will be kind to you.'

All the way home, waiting for the bus that never came, and eventually resigning herself to the long wet walk, Robin's tired mind flitted between the miserable little room and memories of her own early childhood, when the loss of her pretty Polish mother had been raw.

Back in the icy bathroom in her digs, coaxing the recalcitrant geyser into life, Robin felt a stab of longing for Plas Gwyn, her home in the Golden Valley of Armishire. She loved her settlement work, and she had fought hard to be allowed to do it; but at times like this it would have been wonderful to come home to a bit of Jo's cosseting. She huddled deeper into her orange dressing gown, watched the sullen trickle of water into the tub, and wished that the ache in her chest would wear off.

'It's just sadness,' she told herself. 'That awful room—and Frau Gradl can't be very old—probably only Jo's age. And Sabine—the kindest orphanage in the world can't make up for losing your mother. But I wish I'd been able to comfort her the way Sister Bernadette did. She's not so very old either.'

The water reached the line painted round the bath by the landlady. Robin sighed, turned off the tap, and lowered herself into the lukewarm water.

\*

Robin was unable to fulfil her promise to visit Sabine. The hours in wet clothes took their toll on a constitution never robust, and for long days and painful nights she shivered, burned and coughed in the throes of a sharp attack of the bronchitis.

Frau Gradl had been sleeping in the churchyard for two weeks before Robin was 'sitting up and taking notice', as Jo put it. Jo had wanted to nurse Robin herself, in the girl's own pretty bedroom at Plas Gwyn, but her husband Jack, after examining Robin, had vetoed this, and insisted on carrying her off to the San in the Welsh mountains.

'You know what a wholesale creature you are, Jo. You'll wear yourself out nursing her.'

Jo made a face. 'But Jack—my Robin!'

'She'll be better off at the San. I'll see her every day—and of course you can visit her. But nursing I won't allow, and you'll jolly well have to do what you're told for once.'

And with that, Jo was forced to be content.

Now, in the sunny private room with its view over heathery hills, she surveyed her adopted sister. Robin was naturally slight, but the hand that held the crochet hook—for Robin hated to be idle and had begged for her work as soon as she felt able—was thin, and the shoulders in the soft pink bed-jacket were surely narrower than usual. Even more worrying, Robin's face was unusually grave, and it seemed to Jo that there was an unhappy, troubled look in the brown eyes, which she had never seen there before. Only the rampant dark curls, brushed loosely back and tied with a ribbon, were as luxuriant as ever.

'You look,' quoth Jo, 'like something the cat dragged in.' But her black eyes were soft with love and anxiety.

'I'm all right.' Robin's deft fingers fluttered as the tiny green square of crochet in her hands grew.

'What a pretty colour!'

'It's for Sister Bernadette—at the orphanage, you know. They have such a lot of children and some of them arrive with nothing.

I hope you don't mind. But your children have so much—'

Joey bent to kiss the pale forehead. 'Don't be a juggins! Of course I don't mind. It's good to see you taking an interest in something again.'

Robin smiled for the first time, but talking so much brought on the troublesome cough, and it was some minutes before she recovered herself. For the rest of the visit Jo forced herself to keep up a bright chatter about the children and the Chalet School, and Robin needed to do nothing except smile and nod. But the crochet lay untouched on the coverlet, and when Jo bent to kiss her goodbye she noticed that Robin's cheek was hot.

Cold fingers of dread squeezed Jo's heart as she sought her husband in his consulting room.

'Jack—Robin shouldn't still be so pulled down, surely? I thought you and Jem were happier about her these days, but she seems so frail …' Her voice died away as she saw the gravity on Jack's face. 'Oh Jack, I can't bear it! Not my Robin!'

Jack took her in his arms. 'Now, Jo, you mustn't upset yourself so. Jem gave Robin a thorough overhaul yesterday. And no—she isn't quite as well as we'd hope. But,' he added, as Jo trembled, 'Jem believes, and I do too, that it's simply the result of working too hard. And such work.'

'We never wanted her to do settlement work! She needn't work at all. She knows that—there's a home for her at Plas Gwyn, and plenty to do in the nursery. She mustn't wear herself out in the East End. I won't allow it, Jack!'

'Robin, my good girl, is an adult. You can't prevent her doing anything. Oh, I agree she mustn't go back to Bethnal Green. And I rather gather she'd been helping out with a tubercular case. It's rife, of course—the overcrowding, and the damp.' He frowned. 'We've made such strides in recent years, but the poor—well, they don't stand a chance.'

'Jack—you don't think Robin—?'

'No-o-o.' Jack Maynard's face was serious. 'But there are symptoms I don't like, and I don't want her at Plas Gwyn. No, Jo, don't look like that. I don't fear infection. But it's too relaxing for her. She needs bracing air.'

'She was always better in the mountains,' Jo said, thinking of the beautiful Tirolean home where Robin, as a frail motherless child, had thriven. 'If only we could send her to the Sonnalpe.'

'No use wishing that, I'm afraid—Austria's going to be out of bounds for some time by the look of things. No, Rob will get the best possible care here, though it might be a longer pull than we'd hoped. Now, Jo, I've asked Davidson to run you to the station. I don't want you late home; you've had enough broken nights with Michael and it won't help anybody if you get overtired.'

'What a fusser you are, Jack,' groaned Jo, as she lifted her face for his kiss, but she had to own he was right: the shock of seeing Robin so ill had worn her out, and it would be some hours before she was safely back in Plas Gwyn. 'But I'll come again next week and you must promise you'll ring me up at once if she … if she gets any worse. Oh, Jack! I wish I didn't feel so helpless!'

'I know, my dear, but don't forget there *is* a way you can help Robin. Chin up, Joey darling—God willing, Robin will be fit and strong again, though she'll have to say goodbye to her work, of course.'

'Well, that's one good thing to come out of this,' retorted Jo as she pulled on her big coat. 'Goodbye, Jack. I know you're doing all you can for Robin—the rest is in God's hands.'

*

A few days after Jo's visit, as Robin lay listlessly back on her pillows watching the sun sink behind the western hills and the early dusk of December seep up the valley, there was a knock at her door. She turned in surprise, for supper was not due for another hour, nor was she expecting any visitor.

'Miss Humphries, there's a Miss Burthill on the telephone,' said the little red-headed nurse. 'She's most insistent she speaks to you. Most insistent.'

'Zephyr!' exclaimed Robin, smiling at the thought of just how insistent Zephyr Burthill could be. 'Oh, *may* I speak to her, Nurse, please?'

'If you wrap up well and don't talk for more than five minutes, the doctor says you may.'

Robin pulled on dressing-gown and slippers, then, flinging a soft woollen shawl over her shoulders, for the evening was chilly with the promise of frost, hurried down the stairs to the big office where the telephone was.

Zephyr's voice came clearly down the line. 'Robin? Oh Robin, you poor dear, I had no idea you'd been so ill! I've been trying to get hold of you for almost a week, and then yesterday your landlady told me you were here and I've been so worried. How are you?'

'Much better, thank you. I'm convalescing really, but I can't go to Jo as she's supposed to be taking things easy just now, and it would be too damp at The Witchens, and Madge has some doctor friends of Jem's staying, so Jack thinks it's best if I stay here till—till I get my strength back.'

Her voice wobbled slightly on those last words, but Zephyr did not appear to have noticed, for she burst in eagerly, 'Convalescing? Really? You're not still getting medicine or injections or anything beastly like that?'

'Nothing like that. Oh, I'm supposed to rest every afternoon and they're feeding me up like the Christmas goose, but there's no actual treatment now.'

'But this is wonderful! And yesterday I thought I'd have to give up the whole idea!'

'Zephyr Burthill, stop talking in riddles and tell me what on earth you mean!'

'Well, it's like this: Larry and Daphne Foulds, and Peter Cavendish and a few others are planning a trip to Switzerland in the New Year for the winter sports, and I'd got Daddy to agree that I could go with them as long as you came too. He thinks an awful lot of you, you know. I've been trying to ring you for days to see if you'd like to come, but then when I heard you were so ill, I thought … but now—well—where better to convalesce than the Alps? Oh Robin, surely Dr and Mrs Maynard would let you come?'

'They'll forbid me to do any winter-sporting of course, but I really think they may jump at the idea of Switzerland,' replied Robin, picturing the beautiful Tirolean mountains where she had spent so many happy years before the Nazi invasion of Austria had forced them to flee. She felt pierced with a sudden longing to breathe pure Alpine air again, to feel the powder-fine snow beneath her feet and drink in the glorious winter sunsets when the peaks were bathed in a saffron glow. 'I know they've wished I could go somewhere like that, but they didn't want to send me off on my own and we just couldn't see any way of managing it—this could be the perfect solution.'

'Is Jack there? Can you ask him at once? I want this settled immediately! Oh, Robin, it will be such fun!'

'Jack's down in the village at the moment, but I'll ask him as soon as he gets back. I'd better go now; I don't want to get on the wrong side of the nurses, but I'll ring you up as soon as I've spoken to Jack.'

'Good luck! Ring me pronto with good news!'

Alone in her room, Robin collapsed into her armchair and gave herself up to a paroxysm of coughing. It was not far to the office, but in her weakened state even the smallest exertion took its toll. When the attack had passed she picked up her crochet, but her mind was too full to concentrate on her work and presently she let it fall to her lap while she gazed out at the valley, where lights now twinkled cheerily from the houses in the village. She could not have said quite why, but at the prospect of going to Switzerland a shoot of hope had begun to push through the despair she had been battling against since realising she could not return to the work on which she had set her heart. 'I must go,' she thought. 'Jo and Jack are kindness itself, but I need to be on my own, away from everything, so I can think clearly. And try to find out what I'm to do with my life now, for it's not enough just to make my home with Jo or Madge. Oh, I know that's what Jo would like, and I hate to disappoint her, but she has Jack and the children—she doesn't really need me; and I feel I'm meant to be somewhere where I'm truly needed, where I can make a real difference. Only where that is, I—I'm not sure yet.'

For some reason, her mind flew back, as it did so often these days, to Frau Gradl's miserable room, and the kindly Irish nun stroking Sabine's hair while her soft voice calmed them all in the well-loved words of the rosary. But she pushed the thought aside—the doctors had warned her often that dwelling on sadness would not help her recovery—and turned determinedly back to the pleasanter prospect of Switzerland.

'Zephyr and her friends will be out most of the time ski-ing and skating,' she thought, 'and I can go for walks alone in the mountains and … well, I think the answer might come to me more easily there.'

At this point in her reverie, the door opened to admit one of the little Welsh maids with her supper tray, and for the first time since that awful day in Frau Gradl's room Robin eyed the dainty meal with appetite.

'That looks delicious, Bronwen,' she said. 'Goodness, I feel hungry this evening!' She took a long drink from the glass of milk before picking up her fork and setting to work on a plate of freshly scrambled eggs, and the nurse, arriving later to collect the tray, was met, much to her delight, with clean glass and plates. The healing which the life-giving Alpine air would bring had already, in some small measure, begun.

*

Robin threw open the window of the bedroom she shared with Zephyr and leaned out, breathing in the crisp Alpine air and gazing at the panorama of white peaks rising above the dashing black river just below her balcony. From the small hotel where she had been ensconced with Zephyr and her friends for the last week, she could not see or hear the gay winter sports on the high slopes above the village, but she knew from the bright eyes and reddened cheeks of the jolly crowd when they returned at teatime each day that they were thoroughly enjoying themselves.

'As am I,' Robin told herself aloud, pulling the window to and securing the catch, for the little Swiss maids tended to be horrified if they came in to find the cold mountain air blowing through the bedroom. 'It's wonderful to be back in the Alps, and feeling so much better.'

At Jem and Jack's insistence, she was rising late and resting in the afternoons, and the ski-ing and tobogganing of the others were forbidden her just yet, but she was having a pleasant time walking by the river, in the hotel gardens, and around the neat little village which, with its gay-frescoed chalets and steep snowy paths, reminded her so much of her beloved Tirol.

'It's all jolly; just a little—well, I don't think I realised quite how alone I'd be.'

Then, with a determined shake of her slim shoulders, she gathered up her crochet and her book and sought the morning room, which she generally had to herself. At this time of year the Hotel der Fluss catered almost exclusively for winter sporters, who tended to be out all day. Today, however, when Robin pushed open the door into the pretty pine-panelled room, with its panoramic view down the snowy valley, she found someone already in possession of the armchair which she had come to regard as hers.

At her entrance, he sprang to his feet. 'Miss Humphries,' he said. 'I do hope I shan't be disturbing you.'

Of all Zephyr's friends, Peter Cavendish was the one with whom Robin felt least comfortable. The girls were not exactly kindred spirits but they were easy enough company. The other young men were more like the Bettany boys, or David Russell—teasing and jolly. She felt years older than them though she was much the same age. But Peter was a little older—old enough, she knew, to have served in the war—and rather distant in his manner. So she was slightly dismayed to find herself obliged now to talk to him—for of course she could not leave, nor could she pick up her book after a few pleasantries, as she might have done with a stranger. But she smiled as warmly as she could.

'Mr Cavendish. I was just thinking I should like a little company. But why aren't you ski-ing?'

'Oh.' He looked uncomfortable. 'I—well, I overslept.'

Robin laughed. 'It's the air. I always sleep like a baby in the Alps.'

'Always? You've been here before?' His rather grave face lit up with interest.

'Not Switzerland.' She sat down in the chair opposite Peter's and automatically began to crochet the latest little blanket for Sister Bernadette. 'But I spent much of my childhood in the Tirol—Austria, you know.'

'Austria?' His face darkened. 'Yes, I—I was there during the war.'

Robin waited for him to say more, but after a moment he turned slightly and looked intently out of the window, a little muscle twitching in his jaw.

'Why, he looks tired to death,' Robin realised, with a little throb of sympathy. Not for nothing had she been a much-loved and caring head-girl, not to mention her experience in the East End slums. 'Mr Cavendish—forgive me, but—are you quite well? You look rather ...' ('... like something the cat dragged in,' she thought, and smiled at the memory of Jo. She was more tactful than Jo, however.) 'Rather tired,' she fell back on.

Cavendish shook his head. 'I'm quite all right, Miss Humphries. I didn't sleep awfully well, that's all.'

Robin opened her mouth to protest—had he not said that he had overslept?—but a look of strain in the reddened grey eyes reminded her suddenly of how her own face had looked in the mirror at her Bethnal Green digs, those mornings after her last visit to the Gradls, when she had dragged herself up after nights of coughing and struggling to breathe.

'I understand,' she said simply. 'Shall I ring for Kaffee? And then—I wonder if you'd like to walk by the river? The air's awfully fine—just the ticket if your head's aching.'

'Well—it is rather,' Cavendish admitted. 'Silly, really.'

After a basket of the bread twists so familiar to Robin from her schooldays, and a cup each of luscious Swiss coffee, Robin fetched coat and cap and they set off through the hotel gate to the path that bordered the river.

'Christmas card land, my sister Jo used to call it,' said Robin, pausing for a moment to drink in the beauty of the scene; the snow sparkling in the sun, and the brightly painted chalets a splash of colour against the dazzling white. 'How I wish all those kiddies in the East End could come here. They've never seen anything like this, only dirty London slush, and the air would do them so much good.'

Cavendish followed her gaze. 'Yes; it almost seems wasted on us somehow, who are used to good things and have no real need … Miss Humphries, forgive me, I know how ill you've been.'

'And how lucky I am to be able to come here to convalesce,' retorted Robin quickly. 'You're right, Mr Cavendish—'

'Oh, Peter, please,' he interrupted.

'Well, only if I can be Robin. It often strikes me how "ill-divid" the world still is, and how little one seems able to do to make it better.'

Peter turned to her in surprise. 'How can you, of all people, think that? You do more to "make it better" than anyone I've ever known. Zephyr's told me—well, quite a bit about you.'

Robin smiled wearily. 'I used to hope I could be of some use, but now … well, things don't always work out the way we plan, do they?'

'No.'

They turned back to the path and began to walk beside the river, their feet crunching on the dry, powdery snow, for although the path was swept every morning, a brief flurry while they had been having their coffee had left a fresh dusting.

'I know what you mean about things not working out as one expects,' said Peter after a few moments. 'I expect you know my brother was killed at El Alamein.'

'Zephyr told me,' said Robin, her brown eyes warm with sympathy. 'I'm so sorry—for you and your parents.'

'Yes … well. Pretty rotten all round, really. Poor old James. And it leaves me as the only son, which means I'm going to have to inherit the family estate—not at all the sort of life I had envisaged.' He turned his face away, but not before Robin had seen the look of bleak misery in his eyes.

'But you will have work to do, worthwhile work, helping to build the country up again after the war,' she replied.

'Yes—I try to look at it like that, but … it's just that it's all rather different from what I'd been hoping for. Or what I used to hope for, before the war. I'd virtually decided, you see, before I joined up, to go in for missionary work, but then—'

'Oh, Peter! I do understand how terribly hard it is to have to give up something like that.'

'I rather thought you might.' He turned to her with a crooked smile. 'Most people thought it was crazy, but I had a feeling you might see.'

Robin chose her words carefully. Her faith went deep, and she always found it hard to talk of such things, but recently she had spent much thought and prayer on trying to understand what God wanted from her, and this, and her real desire to help her new friend, made the words come more easily.

'But don't you think,' she said, 'that if a door like that is closed to us, then another must be opened? God wouldn't give you a call like that and then prevent you from acting on it if He didn't have a good reason for it. He must have something important for you to do at home.'

'Yes. Oh, I know that's how I should see it, but … I'm just not sure any more. I seem to have lost that sense of purpose—that absolute certainty I used to have that what I was doing was right.'

'I think maybe—well, perhaps God doesn't always give us what we *think* is right.' She struggled to say what she meant. 'But maybe He always gives us what is best for us and the grace to realise it, if—well, if we can truly trust in Him.' Robin raised her brown eyes to meet Peter's grey ones.

'I wish—I wish I could think like you,' said Peter in a low

voice, before lapsing into silence. 'I did once, but … well, it doesn't matter. Are you cold, Miss Hu— I mean Robin? Shall we walk into the village or do you want to turn back?'

They continued their walk, and the conversation turned to lighter matters. By the time they returned to the hotel Robin was surprised to find how much she had enjoyed Peter's company. By mutual consent they agreed to meet up again the following day, and soon a routine had been established whereby they spent most of their days together, enjoying the fresh Alpine air and finding, perhaps, as much comfort in each other's understanding as in the sublime landscape.

*

'You certainly seemed to have cheered old Peter up,' remarked Zephyr one evening almost a week later, when she and Robin were in their bedroom changing for dinner. 'Larry says he hasn't seen him in such terrifically good form for aeons! What magic have you been working?'

Robin laughed as she twisted the curly tail of dark hair into a loose bun at the nape of her neck. 'Goodness, I'm no magician— but he's awfully nice, you know, when you get to know him, not at all as stern and stiff as he looks.'

Zephyr studied her face in the mirror and dabbed some more powder on her nose. 'Heavens, I think I'm getting sunburnt! Well, Larry says he's grinning like a Cheshire cat these days, and they'd all begun to think he'd never smile again, poor man.'

'He's been through a lot.' Robin sat down on her bed, and watched Zephyr searching amongst her extensive selection of face creams and make-up.

'Of course, it was ghastly about his brother,' continued Zephyr. 'And then he was badly wounded himself and in hospital for months, but Larry and Jack think it's more than that somehow. They've tried to get him to talk about it, but he just closes up and won't say a word. I say, do you think this lipstick goes with my frock?'

Robin considered politely, although she would have been the first to acknowledge her lack of expertise on the matter of make-up. 'Oh yes, I think so. Peter's talked about his brother, of course, and the estate, and how he's never wanted that sort of life, but I've wondered myself if there wasn't something … more.' Robin gazed unseeingly at Zephyr's reflection in the mirror. 'For one thing, I'm sure he's not sleeping properly, even though we're in the fresh air as much as possible, but when I try to talk to him about it he always manages to change the subject.'

'Well, it's not all gloom, you know.' Zephyr outlined her lips in deep crimson. 'He'll be rich as Croesus when his father dies, and Brooklands is absolutely beautiful. Do you know it?'

Robin shook her head.

'It's practically a mansion, Elizabethan, with a maze in the grounds and acres of parkland and that sort of thing. Old Peter will be quite the catch one of these days!' Zephyr spun round on the stool to face Robin. 'Oh my goodness—I've just had the most amazing idea! It's almost as though it's Meant To Be!'

'What on earth are you talking about?'

'You and Peter, of course!'

'What about me and Peter?'

'Well, you get on frightfully well together—he likes you tremendously, I know—and you're interested in the same sort of things—good works and all that—and he's quite handsome really, especially when he smiles, and now that you won't be able to work any more … well, it would be perfect!'

'Oh, Zephyr, don't! Please. I wish you wouldn't talk like that.'

A glance at Robin's face made the colour flood into thoughtless

Zephyr's cheeks. 'But I didn't mean any harm—I only meant that you and Peter would make the most lovely couple, and I should be so happy to have you married—I only thought of it because I'm so fond of you both! Oh Robin, please don't look like that!'

'I'm sorry—I don't mean to sound priggish but—well, I believe marriage is a private and … and sacred thing, Zephyr, not something to be gossiped and giggled about,' Robin stammered in some confusion. 'I'm going down to dinner now. Please let's not talk about this again.'

It was the next morning before Robin had regained her normal composure, but she was annoyed to find herself oddly constrained and shy when Peter joined her in the salon after breakfast. 'Oh dear,' she thought, as they walked along the path in what did not feel to her like their usual comfortable silence. A glance at Peter showed that something was badly wrong with him too; his face was grey with exhaustion and the muscle in his jaw was twitching again. Suddenly anxious lest his friends had been talking to him as Zephyr had to her, she gathered her courage and asked, her voice barely audible over the rushing of the water, 'What's wrong, Peter?'

'I've had a letter from home,' he said. 'Afraid the pater's rather rotten. He's never been the same since James—and Mother thinks I ought to be at home just now.'

'I'm so sorry. I hope your father will recover.' Robin was annoyed to feel the flush in her cheeks at the sudden unbidden memory of Zephyr's unguarded words about Peter's inheritance.

'He's much older than Mother,' Peter said. 'Oh, he isn't really ill but there's no doubt he isn't quite up to his duties on the estate. I've always known the time would come when I … well, when I should have to go and start doing my bit. It seems perhaps that time is now. I shall have to see about trains.'

'I shall miss our walks,' Robin said softly, and again felt that unaccustomed self-consciousness.

'And I.' Peter sighed. 'Robin,' he said, 'may I speak to you of something—well, rather private?'

A little ribbon of fear wound itself round Robin's heart. Surely Peter wasn't going to be sentimental?

'Of course,' she said with a swift silent prayer for guidance.

Peter looked up at the towering mountains above them, streaks of grey scree scarring the glistening white of the jagged peaks above the ski slope. 'It's a wonderful landscape, isn't it?' he began. 'So beautiful but so cruel.'

'It helps you to understand the—the bigness of everything,' Robin agreed.

'I told you I'd been to Austria in the war?'

'Yes?' Robin wasn't quite sure where Peter's thoughts were leading but was relieved that they didn't, for now, seem to be dwelling on anything romantic.

'Have you heard of Mauthausen, near Linz?' His face twisted as if he found the name hard to pronounce.

'I don't believe—oh! Yes, of course.'

'It was a death camp. I was with the liberating army.'

Robin's hand flew to her mouth. 'Oh, Peter! How—how dreadful.' She thought of Onkel Florian, the father of two of her schoolmates, Gisela and Maria Marani. He had perished in a Nazi camp early in the war and there was reason to believe that others of their German and Austrian friends who had never been accounted for had met similar fates.

'It changed everything.' Peter's voice shook a little, and he frowned, and turned slightly away, resting one hand on the iron rail which protected the path at this point.

Robin could see how difficult it was for him to speak of this. Yesterday, perhaps, she might have put a comforting, chummy hand on his arm, but today the memory of Zephyr's words made her shy.

'One had heard, of course, about the camps—but to see those people—to see the evil that men can do. And to know that God—well, it made Him seem very far away. I still can't—'

'You dream of it still,' Robin stated with a sudden flash of insight.

Peter's cheeks flushed. 'Yes. It's been … better … out here, especially since … well, our talks have helped. But sometimes … even hearing people speak German—' He gave a little shudder. 'The worst of it is,' he went on, 'that I don't have the—the right to be so haunted by it. I was only a witness, really.'

'You were more than a witness, if you helped to liberate Mauthausen.'

'Well—I was only doing my job. But what you said last week—about God always calling us to what is best for us, even if we can't see it ourselves, and giving us the grace to follow it through as well. You see, after Mauthausen I couldn't even believe in God at all. After seeing that kind of suffering … But what you said—well, it helped more than you'll ever know. I'd been—I suppose I was angry with Him.' He frowned. 'I still can't pretend to understand, but I—I know that I need to have faith in Him.' His voice thickened with emotion. 'I hadn't been able to pray since—oh, for a long time. And then—since last week, I find I can. It helps. But now, going back to Brooklands, which I know I'll have to, looking after things there—it still doesn't seem enough.'

'What sort of work will you do there?' Robin asked, wisely focusing on practical things, though somewhere inside her thrilled at the fact that she, Robin Humphries, had helped this decent young man find his way back to faith. She pulled her coat round her, for a chill rose from the glacial waters of the river.

'It's a big estate. There are some farms and a village—rather feudal, I suppose, these days. The parents expect me just to keep things ticking along the way they always have. And I do love the old place. It's just that increasing the barley yield and making sure the cottage roofs are in order—it doesn't seem enough.'

'I should think it's rather important to the cottagers to have a landlord who cares about their roofs,' retorted Robin, remembering the grinding poverty of some of the Tirolean peasants round the Tiernsee, where she had spent part of her girlhood.

To her delight, Peter laughed and some of the strain left his face. 'Yes. But I had imagined myself abroad—Africa or India. Really changing lives. And then— Well, after Mauthausen I didn't even want that any more. All my certainties had been destroyed. I've been drifting, not settling to anything, trying to distract myself.'

'But you can't drift any longer,' Robin said firmly. 'And if you're going home with renewed faith—that's wonderful. I'm sure God will help you see how you can do His work—and it won't just be cottage roofs.'

'No.' Peter looked at his hand, and then, as if making up his mind to something, lifted it from the rail and took up Robin's small, woollen-mittened hand in his.

'Oh,' she thought. 'No, please, don't be sentimental.'

'Robin. We've become such pals. I—I had hoped to have longer here before asking you, but I must start for home almost at once, and I—I can't leave without being sure. I think you know what I mean.'

Robin bit her lip. She remembered Jo saying how she suddenly knew she cared for Jack; remembered other married friends saying how they felt. She didn't feel that way at all.

'Peter, please—I don't—please don't—' she murmured.

'I've never talked to a woman as I can talk to you,' he rushed on, suddenly boyish in his eagerness. 'You're so jolly understanding. I've been thinking about what you said—about the East End kiddies, and God having work for me. There'd be space at Brooklands to build a holiday home—think what a difference a few weeks in the country would make to them. Oh, Robin, darling Robin, say you'll do it. You've helped me see what kind of work I could do, but I wouldn't want to do it without you by my side.'

Robin was so moved that she had to turn away so Peter would not see her face. 'Peter,' she began. 'I'm terribly, terribly fond of you. You've helped me too, you know. I was feeling rather adrift myself since I had to give up my settlement work.'

'This would be the next best thing! Better, surely? I love you, Robin—I can't help loving you, and I'd care for you—oh, Robin, give me the right to care for you.'

Tears filled Robin's eyes. 'I can't. I don't think I can explain. I feel … I don't feel that I shall ever marry.'

'I know you haven't been fearfully strong,' Peter said. 'And if—well, if you think it wiser not to have children of our own, we could adopt. I shouldn't mind. I'm not so beastly feudal as all that. There are thousands of orphaned children all over Europe. You've told me of that little girl, Sabine, in the orphanage. We could—'

'Peter. Please! Don't!' Robin cast her eyes up to the snowy peaks, hoping for some kind of inspiration to help her say what she needed to say. For of course the picture he painted was delightful—it would be a useful life, and a pleasant one.

But it wasn't what God wanted for her.

All the disappointments of the last few months—her guilt at being unable to comfort Sabine, her shame at breaking down and being unable to continue the work she loved, her vague feeling that the protected and cherished life she could have in Jo's household would never be enough—receded, and the path ahead of her, like the little mountain stream below them which carved a clean, dark passage through the snow, was clear.

'Peter.' She tried again. 'I shall never marry. I'm not just saying that to soften the blow. I feel—I think, deep down I've always felt, but I wouldn't admit it to myself—that God wants something very different from me.' It was too soon to speak of what she meant, but she could see, beyond the hurt in Peter's grey eyes, the beginnings of understanding. 'You said I helped you. If I have, I'm awfully pleased. I've felt rather helpless lately. And knowing I've helped you—well, that's what's finally made me see what I want—what God wants. And it's—it's the same thing.'

Her hand was still in his, and she pulled it away, but very gently. 'Oh, Peter, you can understand, can't you? We could neither of us be happy if we felt we were going against God.'

'He brought us here, together,' Peter protested. 'How can you be so sure this isn't what He wants?'

'I just know. Yes, He brought us here and it was so we could be shown the path He wants us to take, but He doesn't mean us to walk that path together. I shall always think of you as a friend, a dear friend, and I'll pray for you as long as I live—but we both have work to do, and we have to go and do it.'

Peter was silent. His eyes were fixed again on the mountain peaks but Robin knew he was not really seeing them.

'I can't bear this,' she thought. 'I've hurt him and it's the last thing I would ever want to do, but I can't give him what he asks. Oh, I hope he meets someone who can really make him happy; but it's not me, it can't be. I know now what my life is to be.' And, in spite of her distress, joy swelled in her heart, a joy as great, perhaps greater, than any that could ever have come to her from any human love.

A touch on her arm brought her back to the present.

'Robin—it's all right.' Peter's voice was low, but the eyes looking into hers, although dark with misery, held no trace of anger or resentment. 'I do understand. I wish it could be otherwise, but I understand. You've helped me find my way back to God—I can't do anything to take you away from Him. I love you, Robin, but—' He broke off abruptly and turned away. 'I'll see you back at the hotel.' His voice was unsteady and he set off at a brisk pace along the path that led up the mountain.

Robin watched until she could barely make him out, a dark outline against the white, before realising with a shiver that she had stood in the cold much longer than Jem or Jack would have approved of, and hastened back to the hotel. Her heart ached for Peter, but she could not be unhappy on her own account, for now all the pieces of her life seemed to have come together to make a perfect whole, a completeness that she had never thought would be hers.

'I must go home too,' she thought, 'I must tell Sister Bernadette. And then—and oh, I hope I can make her understand—then I must tell Jo.'

Robin ran up the steps to the hotel door. She paused for a moment to look up at the mountains and breathe a wordless prayer of gratitude.

The way ahead would not always be easy, and there would be sadness as well as joy, but the call was now too strong to be ignored, and in answering it at last she was already beginning to find a peace and contentment that, though she could not know it then, would be with her for the rest of her life.

# MEET THE AUTHORS

## Sheena Wilkinson and Susanne Brownlie

Sheena and Susanne met in 1996 after Sheena put an advertisement in the Friends of the Chalet School magazine, looking for local Chalet fans. At the time Sheena was busy with the PhD thesis which became *Friends in the Fourth* (Bettany Press 2007), while Susanne was busy in the more traditional EBD sense with a new baby. Sheena is now an award-winning author of young adult novels at which Miss Annersley would be truly shocked. Susanne is now the mother of three young adults by whom Miss Annersley would also be shocked—the youngest of whom is Sheena's godchild.

Never before having met fellow collectors, they indulged in much swapping of books and opinions and the discussion of such vital topics as which Chalet girls they would invite to tea, and whether the death of Jack, the brindle bulldog in the Little House books, is sadder than Auntie's letter in *Gay from China at the Chalet School.* Susanne introduced Sheena to Elsie Jeanette Oxenham's Abbey girls, and in return Sheena initiated Susanne into Dorita Fairlie Bruce and the Anti-Soppists.

*Robin Heeds the Call* is the result of these years of conversation and friendship. For two women as strong-minded as Mary-Lou, Sheena and Susanne found it surprisingly easy to collaborate on this story; a testament to the fully-realised world created by EBD.

# Girls Gone By Publishers

 Girls Gone By Publishers republish some of the most popular children's fiction from the 20th century, concentrating on those titles which are most sought after and difficult to find on the second-hand market. Our aim is to make them available at affordable prices, and to make ownership possible not only for existing collectors but also for new ones, so that the books continue to survive. We also publish some new titles which fit into the genre.

Authors on the GGBP fiction list include Margaret Biggs, Elinor Brent-Dyer, Dorita Fairlie Bruce, Patricia Caldwell, Gwendoline Courtney, Monica Edwards, Josephine Elder, Elizabeth Goudge, Lorna Hill, Clare Mallory, Phyllis Matthewman, Violet Needham and Malcolm Saville.

We also have a range of non-fiction titles, either more general works about the genre or books about particular authors. Our titles/ subjects include *The Chalet School Encyclopaedia*, *Heroines on Horseback*, Girl Guiding, and Monica Edwards and her books. The non-fiction books are in a larger format than our fiction, and they are lavishly illustrated in black and white.

For details of availability and when to order, see our website or write for a catalogue to GGBP, 4 Rock Terrace, Coleford, Radstock, Somerset, BA3 5NF, UK.

www.ggbp.co.uk
www.facebook.com/girlsgonebypublishers

**Fostering friendship between Chalet School fans all over the world**

- *Quarterly Magazines over 70 pages long*
- *Sales & Wants Booklets*
- *Ripping Reads (for other books)*
- *A Lending Library of all Elinor Brent-Dyer's books and other titles as well*

For more information send an A5 SAE to
Ann Mackie-Hunter or Clarissa Cridland
4 Rock Terrace, Coleford, Radstock. Somerset, BA3 5NF, UK
focs@rockterrace.org
www.chaletschool.org.uk
Find us on Facebook: www.facebook.com/friendsofthechaletschool